The First Year: A Marble Grant Novel

Ghost Diet & Other Marble Grant Stories

Ashes to Weddings & Other Marble Grant Stories

A Big Twisted Plot & Other Marble Grant Stories

PAKHET JONES

The Big Tom: A Packet Jones Short Novel

Big Eyes: A Packet Jones Short Novel

THUNDER MOUNTAIN

Thunder Mountain

Monumental Summit

Avalanche Creek

The Edwards Mansion

Lake Roosevelt

Warm Springs

Melody Ridge

Grapevine Springs

The Idanha Hotel

The Taft Ranch

Tombstone Canyon

Dry Creek Crossing

Hot Springs Meadow

Green Valley

SEEDERS UNIVERSE

Dust and Kisses: A Seeders Universe Prequel Novel

Against Time

Sector Justice

Morning Song

The High Edge

Star Mist

Star Rain

Star Fall

Starburst

Rescue Two

COLD POKER GANG

Kill Game

Cold Call

Calling Dead

Bad Beat

Dead Hand

Freezeout

Ace High

Burn Card

Heads Up

Ring Game

Bottom Pair

You Forgive The Night's Scream & Other Poker Boy Stories

Dean Wesley Smith

WMG PUBLISHING

Contents

SNEAK PEEK
BEING DEAD (THE FIRST YEAR)

INTRODUCTION

How could I not title one of these new Poker Boy collections with the title of the lead story? What a great title and I have no memory at all of where it came from. Just none.

But I think it fits the first story in this collection perfectly all the way.

I made no attempt to try to put the stories in these collections in any kind of chronological order. Just felt that might be too dull. So in some stories Poker Boy only has limited powers and in others he has more, totally depending on when I wrote the story.

And in some stories there is a team member and later on that team member has moved on and is never mentioned again.

So basically this collection is one of discovery of Poker Boy and Patty and some of his team members. And, of course, the Silicon Suckers, which have been part of the Poker Boy world since the very first story.

Also, the last story in this collection is about Poker Boy's boss, Stan, the God of Poker. We learn a lot about Stan and how long he has been around and his family.

So hope you enjoy these ten Poker Boy adventures as much as I did writing them.

Dean Wesley Smith
Las Vegas, Nevada

You Forgive The Night's Scream & Other Poker Boy Stories

You Forgive The Night's Scream

Chapter One

I woke with the sound of a woman's scream echoing in my head.

High-pitched.

Full of terror.

I sat bolt upright in bed.

My heart pounded like it wanted to get out of my chest and run for the closet and every Poker Boy superpower sense I had was amped up to full power.

Beside me, my girlfriend and sidekick, Patty Ledgerwood, aka Front Desk Girl, lay sleeping soundly, her wonderful long brown hair like a shadow over her pillow in the dim light coming from cracks around the side of the drapes.

Outside, the city of Las Vegas never slept and certainly never turned off its lights. The strip was only a few blocks from Patty's apartment building and my invisible office floated just to the west of her apartment and directly over the MGM Grand Hotel and Casino complex.

I held my breath, waiting for another scream, trying to listen over the pounding of my heart.

Nothing.

A little noise from a truck on the street below Patty's apartment. Then a couple quick beeps as it backed up.

Nothing else.

Yet every danger Poker Boy sense I had was shouting, making me want to get out of there.

That scream had been close, as if it was inside this very apartment. Yet Patty was still sound asleep.

Something was very wrong.

Very wrong.

I've had bad dreams before, but when that scream let go, I have no memory of actually being in a dream.

The scream was real. Outside of my possible dream.

At least real in one fashion or another.

I gently touched Patty's shoulder.

She stirred and rolled to look up at me. "What—"

I put my finger to my lips and shook my head. Then I eased out of bed. I was wearing sweat pants and nothing else. I slipped on my thin brown slippers.

Patty came awake at once, saying nothing and moving silently out of the other side of the bed, slipping on her white bathrobe over her nightgown and her slippers as well.

I stood near the door to the bedroom that led out into the

living room, listening for any noise coming from either the living room or kitchen area.

Silently, Patty came over and touched my arm, using her powers to calm me down some. The pounding of my racing heart subsided and I mouthed the word, "Thanks." One of her super-powers was the ability to keep people calm and focused. I loved it in stressful situations when we worked together. We had discovered that as a team we were far stronger together than apart.

Plus I was head-over-my-slippers in love with her.

She pointed to her ear and shook her head, meaning she was hearing nothing.

I wasn't either, so silently I went out into the living room.

And as I walked ten steps, the temperature of the room dropped a good thirty degrees until suddenly I could see my breath in the dim light.

Patty grabbed my arm and pulled me back into the bedroom, a panicked look on her face.

I'm glad she did. I would need a lot more clothes to go back into that living room.

"Out of time," she whispered and I did, slipping us between instants of time. It felt like I stopped time when I did that, but in reality, time never stopped. I just moved me and Patty inside an instant of time.

Normally, in a busy casino or outside, I could tell instantly when I did that, but in the silent and dark apartment, nothing seemed to change.

"You know what caused that chill?" I asked, shivering as I

tried to warm up a little. All my senses were still screaming that there was danger close by and the memory of that scream seemed to echo in my mind.

I moved over and grabbed a sweatshirt that said "The Golden Nugget Poker Room" and pulled it over my head, easing the chill some.

"Did you hear something?" Patty asked.

I nodded. "A woman's scream. That's what woke me up."

"Oh, no," she said.

Even in the dim light I could tell her face went white.

I glanced up at the ceiling. "Stan. Help!"

Patty nodded and a moment later Stan appeared.

The God of Poker had on what he always seemed to have on. Tan slacks, button down sweater, and loafers. In all the years I had worked for him, I had seldom caught him out of that outfit, day or night.

"Wow," he said, instantly spinning around, looking for the danger. I could feel him strengthen the time bubble and put a shield around us, which helped my screaming warning senses some.

"What is causing that?" he asked.

I shrugged, since I honestly had no idea.

"He heard a scream," Patty said. "In his sleep."

"Oh, shit!" Stan said and instantly vanished, leaving the screen and the stronger time bubble.

I looked at Patty who clearly wasn't in the mood for any of my one-line jokes, so I wisely said nothing. Not a skill I often had, but at the moment with every warning sense I had still going off, it seemed prudent.

Besides, the way they were acting was starting to scare me to death.

The longest five seconds later, Laverne, Lady Luck herself, appeared in our bedroom with Stan and Ben beside her.

Lady Luck didn't have on her normal power business suit, but instead wore a pair of jeans and an old sweatshirt. She looked downright normal for one of the most powerful beings in all the universe.

Ben was a god in the book world that was a member of our team. He looked like a little old librarian and had a perfect memory of everything he had ever read and the history of all the gods.

Lady Luck instantly strengthened the shields around them even more and the sense of warning and fear again decreased but didn't vanish by any means.

"Who heard the scream?" Lady Luck asked.

I sort of half raised my hand.

"Damn it," she said.

Now when Lady Luck swears, you know things can't be good. And I wasn't sure if I wanted to know just how bad things actually were, since all the bad seemed to be focused at me.

Chapter Two

Patty held onto my arm, keeping me as calm as her superpower could manage. But I was feeling anything but calm.

"So what's out there in that cold?" I asked.

"A banshee," Lady Luck said.

Ben nodded, confirming what Lady Luck said but not adding to it.

I almost said that I thought those were myths, but then realized who I was and who was standing around me. I just hadn't been in this superhero business long enough to know what was a myth and what actually had some reality attached to it.

"So tell me exactly what you are worried about," I said.

"The banshee is a fairy that is known to mourn the coming loss of a life," Ben said.

"By screaming?" I asked. "More like it would scare a person to death."

"By screaming," Stan said, nodding. "And the person who hears them is supposed to be the one who will die very shortly. It's both a warning and a sad cry that the person is dying."

Well, I had to admit, I didn't much like the sound of that.

I took a deep breath and could feel Patty's calming influence flow through me. Honestly, over the last few years, I had faced death and the end of the world a few times. And a lot of really tough players in no-limit poker games. So if some being was giving me a warning, I needed to thank her and just flat ask her what was going to happen.

And when.

Never hurt to know when a fella was going to die, I figured.

Seemed so simple. I'm sure there were a dozen reasons it was a stupid idea, but my friends around me just seemed determined to stand next to me when I died and do nothing, so I needed to do something.

And my terrified mind couldn't come up with one other idea. I knew death could follow me anywhere, since I had met two gods of death so far, and sort of liked them both, honestly. So running was out of the question.

I moved over to the closet and pulled out my heaviest Oregon coat. Since I was originally from Oregon and my home casino was in the mountains of Oregon, I at least had a few heavy coats, one of which I had brought to Vegas and stashed in Patty's apartment because at times I had been damned cold here as well.

"What are you doing?" Patty asked, again taking my arm as I came back to her zipping up my parka.

"Going out to talk with the banshee," I said, giving her a quick kiss and heading for the door into the dark living room.

"Not a great idea," Lady Luck said.

I stopped and looked at her. "Has a banshee killed anyone?"

"No, she just warns people," Lady Luck said, her voice sounding sad and tired.

"Then it seems I'll be fine. When was the last time anyone just talked with the banshee?"

Ben shook his head. "There are no records of anyone doing such a thing."

"Five hundred years," Lady Luck said softly.

Ben glanced at her and said nothing. He knew something he wasn't saying.

"Well, if this kills me," I said, doing my best to screw up every ounce of courage I had, "someone tell the next person to not try it."

"I'm coming with you," Patty said.

"No, I heard the scream, I'm the one the banshee is trying to warn."

I glanced at Lady Luck and nodded. I almost said, "Wish me luck" and then stopped as I realized how stupid that really would have sounded to Lady Luck.

Her expression didn't change from extreme seriousness

combined with sadness, something I had never seen on her face.

"While I'm gone," I said, standing near the door of the living room, "someone might want to check with Death, see if I really am on a list at the moment. We did save his ass and help his daughter."

Lady Luck nodded. "I'll do it," she said, and vanished.

I took a deep breath and turned and went into the living room.

The intense cold slapped me and I staggered, but managed to move forward.

"My name is Poker Boy," I said to the cold air, my breath freezing in front of my face. "I heard your scream and came to see if I could help."

Being brash seemed to be the most logical thing I could do.

And that's what people who rescue other people do, after all, go toward the sound of a scream.

"Thank you," a soft female voice said from the other side of the couch.

"Can you stand a little light?" I asked.

"It is not a problem," the voice said.

An instant later the table light beside the couch clicked on. A beautiful and mostly nude small woman sat on the couch under the light. Her skin was a light blue and she had two fragile-looking silver wings tucked behind her.

Her beautiful, long, silver hair cascaded around her and covered most of the important parts.

But there was no two ways about it, she was stunning.

I moved over to a large chair facing her across a frost-covered coffee table and sat down, my hands in my pockets of the heavy ski parka. Somewhere between the door and the chair I had lost touch with my feet, since they were only in thin slippers and I was sure they were already frozen.

"So I assume you were calling me for help?" I asked, doing my best to not push any power toward her for fear she might think I was trying to meddle.

"I was," she said, nodding, moving her silver hair around in such a fashion that any good strip club would hire her in a moment.

"Not warning me like you normally do."

"No, calling you for help," she said.

Relief flooded through me but did nothing to warm me up. You would think it would have.

"I have been stuck in this frigid-state for almost five hundred years now," she said, her voice taking on a little more power. "I have done my job as instructed for five hundred years."

I nodded, a little worried about what was coming next.

"I would like you to help me become free of this punishment."

Oh, great, she's asking the newest member of all the superheroes in God's world for help with something that happened five hundred years ago, as if I should know what that was.

"Why do you think I can help with this?" I asked.

"I have watched you and your team save many, many lives," she said. "I hope you can now save mine."

I nodded. "We can try. But can I bring a few members of my team in here to help me?"

"You can," she said, nodding.

Being afraid to stand on my frozen feet, I shouted to the door. "Patty, Stan, Ben, could you join us?"

She nodded, making her hair dance around the important parts of her body. "I am honored you are willing to try to help me."

Stan had bundled all three of them up in parkas and gloves and they came in slowly like an expedition to the South Pole lost in Patty's apartment. No dog sleds, luckily.

Patty came over and sat on the arm of the chair beside me, calming me some with a touch. Stan and Ben both nodded to the banshee and remained standing.

She nodded back.

I turned back to the banshee and said, "We are ready. Could you tell us what caused this punishment five hundred years ago?"

"It is not punishment for a crime," she said. "It is punishment for love. I loved the wrong woman."

Well, I was as liberal as the next person, but honestly, that answer surprised me, right down to my frozen feet.

Chapter Three

I needed to get this going before I froze completely to the chair. "May I ask first who put this punishment on you?"

I glanced over at Ben who was shaking his head from side-to-side. "You don't want to know," he said softly.

"I did," Lady Luck said, entering the room right after Ben said that.

She did not have a ski parka on and seemed oblivious to the intense cold.

If I got many more surprises like that, the blood actually might reach my feet again.

Patty squeezed my arm to keep me calm.

"How are you, Laverne?" the banshee asked, smiling.

"I am well," Lady Luck said, moving to the end of the

couch and sitting down and facing the banshee. "You are as beautiful as ever."

The banshee nodded her head thank you, again doing wonderful and alluring things with her hair over her perfect blue body.

Who knew a blue body could be perfect?

Then the banshee said something that got me even more confused, which in this frozen state, was going some.

"Thank you for saving my life."

Laverne smiled and nodded. "I am sorry that it had to be in this fashion. It was what your husband would accept as a punishment short of death."

"I have survived," the banshee said. "Loving you was worth it. Is my husband still angry at me?"

"He is not," Lady Luck said. "He is retired, his daughter has taken over his month of duties as Death just last year, and he spends most of his time surfing in Hawaii with his new wife."

I just about choked. This banshee had been married to Death himself. And she had been in love with Lady Luck. Wow, I really needed to spend time with Ben and learn about some of the history of the Gods.

"Then is it possible to return me to the normal world?" the banshee asked.

"I just spoke with your ex-husband," Lady Luck said. "Poker Boy and his team helped his daughter make the transition last year, and I told him that Poker Boy was trying to help you now after five hundred years of punishment."

"Thank you," the banshee said. "He never knew you were the one?"

"He knew," Laverne said. "Right from the start. And he knew it broke my heart, as wells as yours to do what I did. That's why he allowed the punishment."

"I have been wailing over death and broken hearts now for five hundred years," the banshee said. "And with every one I mourned the loss of your love."

"You never lost it," Laverne said.

Once again my toes felt warmer from the shock of that statement.

"You are married, have four grown daughters?" the banshee asked, staring at Laverne in clear surprise.

"My husband and I have," Laverne said, smiling, "shall we say, an open arrangement."

I just about said, "More information than I needed." But my teeth were chattering too much luckily to get that stupid joke out.

Laverne stood and with a "thank you" into the air, more than likely to the banshee's former husband, she waved her hand.

Intense heat filled the room and the banshee sat there, smiling, soaking it all in.

And then finally, after a few seconds, it was over.

I did feel warmer, but not much.

Water was dripping all around Patty's apartment from the melting frost and I could feel the temperature on my face returning to normal, although it would not surprise me to have frostbite on my nose.

The banshee now was no longer blue, but a tanned golden brown all over. And I do mean all over. And her hair was now just as long but a rich brown. And her wings shimmered in a rainbow of colors.

Laverne reached out her hand to the banshee and then said, "Jayne, welcome back."

Jayne took her hand and stood, smiling, her long hair doing little to cover some pretty amazing assets.

"It's a pleasure to be back."

Then Jayne turned to me and said, "Thank you, Poker Boy, and your entire team, for being willing to take a chance on talking to me."

I just nodded, not trusting myself to say anything sane.

"We have some catching up to do," Laverne said, smiling.

"Now that's something I've been looking forward to for five hundred years."

Then, like two teenage girls, they both giggled, and vanished.

Lady Luck giggling was unsettling, to say the least.

Stan shook his head and said, "See you tomorrow."

Then he and Ben vanished.

Patty stood and shivered, water dripping off her coat from the melting frost.

"Would you do me a favor," I asked as she offered to help me out of my chair.

"Anything, my frozen love."

"Would you start a warm shower running. I'm just going to teleport out of these clothes and into the shower from here. I don't think my feet will carry me."

She laughed. "I'll be there, naked, standing under the hot water, ready to catch you."

And she did.

And I got real warm, real quick. I'll leave it at that.

THE WAR OF POKER

The War of Poker

I was starting to figure out that if I wanted a new case or some problem to come up threatening the world and everything I knew, all I had to do was stand in the main lobby of the Las Vegas MGM Grand. Someone, some problem, somehow would find me.

At the moment I really didn't want a new case, but I had learned as a superhero that people needing help or problems needing solving didn't happen when I wanted them to. Annoying, but true.

But even though it might lead to the end of everything I knew, I often spent time in the MGM Grand lobby wearing my black leather coat and black Fedora-like hat that was my superhero uniform, leaning against the same marble pillar, waiting for my girlfriend and sidekick, Patty Ledgerwood, aka Front Desk Girl, to get off work.

That I stood there was common knowledge and also might have something to do with people and problems being able to find me. Superheroes are not normally regular in their schedules.

But standing and waiting and sometimes getting cases was worth it as long as the world didn't end. I liked watching the crowds and watching Patty work. Her long brown hair, deep brown eyes, and wide smile always made me feel wonderful. To say I was in love would be an understatement.

The only place I spent more time was in poker rooms. But except for the poker room at Spirit Winds casino in the mountains of Oregon near my doublewide trailer, I seldom played poker in the same casino. My job as Poker Boy, a superhero in the gambling universe, was to help those who needed help and take the money at poker tables from those who needed it taken because of their poor play.

Sometimes the two parts of my job crossed and combined, but usually the money part just paid the expenses for the superhero part.

Technically, since I was a superhero in the poker-playing niche of the universe, I should only be solving problems associated around poker and poker rooms. But over the last few years I had managed to gather a team of superheroes around me from different aspects of the world. As a team, we had become known for solving some of the stranger problems to come along, including saving the entire world from tiny bugs one day, stopping an alien invasion on another adventure, and saving Lady Luck herself yet another day.

When the team got to work, things were never dull.

Patty, who was part of that team, was still fifteen minutes away from getting off work when I sensed a problem coming towards me. I call that sense my "tingly-warning bell" super-power. Sometimes, but not always, I know when danger is approaching. It's not the kind of power I can trust like Spider-Man trusts his "Spidey-Sense." I often wished my power was that dependable. But when I feel that shiver and the tingle go down my spine like a drip of ice water, I have learned to pay attention. Danger is close by.

Right at that moment a river of ice was flowing all over my spine and I shivered like someone had turned up the MGM Grand air-conditioning to the Arctic setting.

I swung around to see the most beautiful woman I had ever seen walking toward me with a smile. She had long brown hair that seemed to just glow in the bright lights of the lobby, wide brown eyes, and a perfect smile. She wore the uniform of the MGM front desk crew and wore it better than anyone had a right to wear a simple white blouse and brown slacks.

In fact, the woman walking toward me looked exactly like my girlfriend, Patty.

I glanced around at the front desk wondering how I had managed to miss Patty leaving work.

I hadn't.

Patty was still standing behind the desk working with a customer. Her hair was still tucked up tight on her head. She never let it down until she got off work.

I spun back to the woman walking at me.

It was Patty all right, walking toward me smiling, giving me that "look" with her big brown eyes that could melt every ounce of resistance I had toward anything.

All I could do was stare.

How could there be two Patty Ledgerwoods?

The ice shivers running around on my back finally snapped me out of my shock and I stepped out of time, freezing everyone around me.

The loud sounds of the nearby casino and people talking and background music all vanished instantly.

I loved the ability to do that. I actually couldn't stop time, but I could pull myself out of the flow of time and into an instant so that it appeared to me that time had stopped around me.

I liked to think of it as me being in a bubble outside of time, but that wasn't right exactly either.

Around me kids were frozen in mid-scream, husbands were stopped in mid-look at another women, bellhops were stopped with a bag halfway onto a cart.

And there were no sounds.

None.

The superpower came in very, very handy and I had learned that when in doubt about anything, I should just get out of the flow of time and give myself some time to think.

I turned toward the front desk again. My girlfriend, Patty, was frozen in mid-sentence behind the front desk of the MGM Grand hotel talking to a woman with a bored-looking husband in bright red shorts. I knew that was Patty. Every-thing about me could sense that was the woman I loved behind the counter.

From the other direction, the woman who looked just like Patty was frozen in mid-stride about ten steps from where I stood. Her smile looked artificial when frozen like that.

And every sense I had told me she was nothing but danger.

Extreme danger.

I went over and walked around her, studying every detail about her.

She was an exact duplicate of Patty, right down to the tiny mole on her neck.

Same height, same shape, everything.

Creepy didn't begin to describe what I was feeling and I quickly went back to my original position. My damn warning power kept making me shiver like I was fighting upwind through a cold snowstorm in nothing but a swimming suit.

I needed help and I needed it now.

As a superhero, I had learned a long time ago that there were many, many things in the world I did not understand. And with that learning I had lost all fear of just calling for help when there was something I flat didn't understand.

Right now I had no idea what was happening, but I knew it couldn't be good. One Patty Ledgerwood was more than enough for me.

I glanced at the ceiling and shouted "Stan! Need help!"

I have no idea why I look up when I am calling out for

Stan, the God of Poker and my immediate boss, but I always do, and he has never failed to show up at once.

And this time was no exception.

He appeared next to me, also out of time. I had no idea how he could do that, jump right into my frozen moment in time and join me, but he had done it in the past so now was not the time to be asking him how. It seemed for the Gods, time was a lot easier to deal with than for us mortals and superheroes.

Stan had on a plain pair of brown slacks and a tan, open-collared dress shirt. His brown hair was perfectly combed as always and you could walk by him a hundred times and never notice him. He was a perfect master of disguise and blending in.

He glanced at the woman who looked like Patty walking toward me, then frowned, something I hated when my boss and the God of Poker did around me.

"That's not Patty," I said. I pointed back at the main desk of the hotel. "That's Patty."

"I know that," he said, only glancing back at the real Patty. He eased toward the imitation Patty slowly and carefully, like trying to sneak up on a sleeping bear.

He was clearly seeing something I was not seeing.

After two steps, he stopped. "We need help. How long can you hold this field?"

"Another half hour," I said, checking in with how I was feeling holding the bubble with me and Stan out of the time stream. I had gotten pretty good at this super power.

Suddenly I could feel that it was slipping.

"Less," I said, now straining to hold the field. "It's slipping."

Stan nodded and focused for a moment.

The field holding us out of time solidified again.

"What caused that?" I asked, trying to catch my breath. It actually felt like I had just run a hundred-meter sprint.

"She did," he said, pointing at the imitation Patty.

Suddenly I could feel the time bubble starting to slip again.

Stan suddenly looked a little panicked and some beads of sweat broke out on his forehead as he too struggled to hold the field.

"She knows what we are doing," Stan said.

I didn't want to know how he knew or how she could know unless she was some God. I didn't want to think about the fact that I had frozen in time a God and she would be angry at me.

Stan moaned and sweat started to run down his neck. I felt like the time bubble I was working to hold now weighed as much as a large truck. No chance I could hold it much longer and as a poker player, there was nothing on the planet more frightening to me than to see the God of Poker sweat and strain.

Stan glanced up at the ceiling. "Burt! Laverne! Help!"

Every ounce of energy I had was going to hold Stan and I out of time at that moment, or I would have just sat down stunned. Stan had just called for Burt, the God of Casino

Operations and Lady Luck herself, the most powerful God I had ever met.

Who or what was this Patty imitator and why had she scared me and Stan so much?

Burt and Laverne appeared next to the now sweat-covered Stan. Burt wore a gray, three-piece silk business suit and his short stature made him look more like a mob boss than a major God. Laverne was dressed in a black pants suit with matching jacket and had her hair pulled back tight.

"What is the..."

Then she saw the Patty imitator and Lady Luck herself actually flushed.

Suddenly the pressure was off holding the time bubble as both Burt and Lady Luck took over, giving Stan and I rest.

My rubbery knees wanted me to slump to the floor and give them a rest, but instead I managed to keep on my feet trying to catch my breath.

"Who is that?" I managed to ask.

"Morrígan," Lady Luck said, walking over around the imitation Patty. "The Phantom Queen as she is often called. And why she is coming to you, Poker Boy, is a mystery."

Now I was officially and formally scared. When Laverne, Lady Luck herself didn't know something, I knew I was in deep trouble. So I didn't ask the next question on my mind... Who was Morrígan?

"I thought Morrígan was only a myth," Stan said, looking very worried. "Right along with her sisters."

I still had no idea who Morrígan was.

"Nope, all three are real," Burt said, looking very worried. "Just not around much these days."

I am sure I looked worried as well, but that was because I had no idea what was going on and because they were all worried and they were far more powerful than I was.

"After Atlantis," Laverne said, "Morrígan pretty much stayed in the Alps and out of any of the world's problems."

"I heard she was around for the two big wars," Stan said. "After all, she is known as the Goddess of War."

Oh, wow, it was *that* Morrígan who stood there frozen looking like my girlfriend. When a very, very old God started pretending to be your girlfriend, things could not be going well.

Laverne shook her head. "Both wars Morrígan stayed in Switzerland, neutral."

"What is she doing in Las Vegas?" Burt asked.

And instant later Morrígan, still looking like Patty, moved and smiled at Laverne as she stepped into our frozen time bubble. "You could just ask me," she said.

"That's why I brought you out of time," Laverne said, her voice cold and as hard as I had every heard Lady Luck sound.

"Nice seeing you again as well," Morrígan said to Laverne.

She might look like Patty, but the voice was nothing like Patty's at all. Patty had a softness to her voice. This imposter sounded harsh with a coldness in every sentence.

Laverne just stared at Morrígan and the stare was returned in kind. There was clearly no love lost between the two women.

After a moment the woman's appearance shifted. The Patty-look sort of melted and formed into a woman who had long, black hair, a very, very thin face with a long, thin nose, and eyes that were cold black. She had on a white pants suit and was as thin as any supermodel I had ever seen. She towered over all of us because not only was she tall, but she somehow managed to stand on six-inch heels.

Laverne said nothing.

Finally Morrígan smiled at Laverne. "Fine, if you want to be that way, I came to ask a favor of Poker Boy."

Morrígan smiled at me, then went back to staring at Laverne.

I figured if my heart was ever going to explode out of my chest at any point in my life, now was the time. I was stunned I hadn't just fainted dead away under that look. The woman was totally terrifying. I hadn't been this scared in any recent memory. And that was with three of the most powerful Gods in existence standing beside me.

"You could have just come to me," Laverne said.

"And you would have agreed?" Morrígan asked, smiling.

"Of course not," Laverne said.

Looks like I was off the hook at least for the moment.

"That's why I had to take a chance on approaching Poker Boy directly," Morrígan said. "But he is as good as his reputation and saw me coming, clearly."

I think I had just been complimented by an enemy of Lady Luck. Not something I would ever want as a poker player.

"So what was the favor?" Laverne asked, her voice perfectly level and very, very cold.

"I wanted him to teach me how to play poker," Morrígan said.

"I assumed as much," Lady Luck said. "Why?"

The idea of teaching that woman anything, let alone poker had my knees week again. I would rather have five guns pointed at my head than do that.

My warning chill was doing tap dances up and down my spine.

Morrígan laughed, but there was no real humor in the laugh and it brought no smiles to anyone around me. It just made the cold shivers on my spine increase. I was shivering so hard from my danger warning sense, it was lucky my foot wasn't pounding on the ground like an excited dog.

I was going to need to figure out a way to turn that warning signal off when I needed to.

"You might know I have been hanging around with Ares lately," Morrígan said.

I wanted to shout *"The God of War!"* But somehow I managed to stay silent.

"I heard you have been living together since the Cuban Missile Crisis," Laverne said.

"Yeah, he got depressed," Morrígan said, "He was so looking forward to that war. He thought it would have been epic. I've been trying to nurse him back to health."

"I'll bet," Laverne said.

"So we've been playing some poker and I'm tired of losing," she said.

"He cheats," Laverne said flatly. "Get a new deck of cards that he has not touched and see how you do."

Morrígan stood there staring at Laverne for a very, very long moment. Laverne just stared back. For a moment I thought they had stepped outside of the time bubble and were frozen in the instant of time like everyone else in the lobby of the MGM Grand.

Then Morrígan smiled a very mean and angry smile and slowly shook her head. "That bastard."

And then she vanished.

It was as if the sun had come out after weeks of rain and I had won the lottery all in one instant. The cold chills that had been running up and down my back suddenly vanished as well.

"I hate her," Lady Luck said.

"But you might want to let her win some now," Burt said, chuckling.

"Yeah, we'll see," Laverne said.

With that they both vanished.

Stan just stood there shaking his head. Then he laughed and turned to me. "Nice job."

"What did I do?" I said, still feeling stunned.

"You saw her coming," he said. "That's amazing. It's not many people who can see through a Banshee's disguise, let along Morrígan's, the war goddess. And you got out of time without her noticing at first. Impressive against a God that powerful."

"And she's living with Ares? Right?" I asked. "The same Ares of war fame?"

"Yup," Stan said, "as long as they keep themselves entertained with each other and out of the spotlight, the planet is a lot safer."

"Until they get mad at each over a poker game," I said, suddenly feeling less hopeful for the survival of the human race.

"Yeah, until that," Stan said, thinking it was funny now.

"And she and Laverne have issues, clearly?" I asked, trying to get my mind wrapped around what had just happened.

"From way, way back," Stan said, laughing. "A long story I'll tell you about sometime, at least the parts I've heard. It predates me by a few hundred thousand years."

He patted me on the back. "Again, great job. Who knows what kind of problem or major war you just avoided."

"Thanks, I think," I said.

He laughed and vanished.

The pounding sounds of the real world came crashing back in around me as he let go of the bubble outside of time. The fine patrons of the MGM Grand Casino and Hotel were back in motion, laughing, talking, and being very human.

And right now that felt wonderful.

I moved over and leaned against the stone pillar, trying to slow down my racing heart. Patty looked up at me and smiled before going back to helping her customer.

Somehow my poker face allowed her to not notice that I had just escaped an encounter with a very dangerous woman. And who knew what else would have happened if Morrígan had gotten to me.

But how in the world was I going to tell Patty what had just happened in an instant in time right in front of her?

She was never going to believe me.

I turned my gaze to the high ceiling of the lobby. "Stan, can you meet me and Patty at the Diner in thirty minutes? Milkshakes are on me. I need help explaining what just happened. I'm still not sure myself."

I could hear a low, rumbling chuckle echo over the noise of the lobby, then his voice, "Sure thing, kid."

Patty looked up and frowned. She clearly had heard Stan's voice as well.

"Long story," I mouthed at her and she frowned, but went back to work with the customer.

A long story that had only taken an instant to happen.

And a story I had a hunch wasn't over just yet. Morrígan playing poker against Ares just couldn't turn out well. If not this century, then maybe next. That was the nature of the war of a poker game.

Especially now that Morrígan wanted to win.

The Empty Mummy Murders

Chapter One

It was a good ten minutes into the conversation over vanilla milkshakes and a side of fries with Scary Mary, as her friends called her and she called herself, before she got to the point.

Scary Mary deserved the name. She had bright red hair tied up so tight on the top of her head that it pulled the skin of her face and scalp upward. She wore more make-up than a bad rodeo clown, and had breasts that must have arrived at the restaurant a good minute ahead of her.

Her tight red dress, if you could call the small piece of cloth covering her largest assets a dress, I'm sure didn't cover her butt when she slid into the leather booth at The Diner. But I didn't look. In Vegas you saw all types, and a long time ago I had learned to not judge a person by their look or a woman by the expanded size of her chest.

Some friend-of-a-friend had given Scary Mary one of my real-world names and told her I might be able to help with her problems.

As Poker Boy, I find people to help in all sorts of ways. Sometimes I find them, sometimes they come to me, sometimes my boss, Stan the God of Poker, assigns me the task of helping someone. It never seems to make any sense how I find the people who need saving, but I do. Just as I find the people at poker tables who need me to take their money. It seems to be a natural way of the world.

I had told Scary Mary to meet me at The Diner in downtown Las Vegas. The Diner serves the best milkshakes on the planet, and the waitress who is always there is Madge, a superhero in the food service business. The Diner is decorated like a fake 1960s diner. I am convinced there were no places in the 1960s that looked anything like The Diner, with records stapled on the walls and photos of Elvis, Marilyn, and James Dean on most walls.

But the booths were comfortable and the milkshakes huge and made like old milkshakes from the 1930s. And it was where my team met when we had a job to plan.

It was two in the afternoon. No one but Madge was with us in The Diner, and she was working up behind the counter. Scary Mary and I were in a booth near the front door. It was a perfect time to get to the bottom of her problem.

Scary Mary kept looking at me in a worried fashion, so I sort of turned on my Trust-Me power and let it wash over her. I had on my black leather jacket and black fedora-like hat that was my superhero uniform, and I could feel the power they gave me drawing from the nearby casinos. It should be more than enough to get Scary Mary to talk.

After a moment she blushed, which looked washed-out next to her blazing-red hair and beside her thick, blue eyeliner and red lipstick.

"You're not going to believe me and I just don't know what you can do to help," she said, her voice deep and throaty.

"Try me," I said, turning up my Trust-Me" power a little and adding a little Empathy power to it as well. "You would be surprised at what I might be able to do."

"That's what my friend in the poker room at the MGM told me. But you just won't believe me."

"Let me decide that," I said.

She signed, looked both directions. "I'm being harassed by aliens."

"Oh, no," I said, sighing and stirring up my milkshake. This felt like a problem I had had three years before with an old girlfriend. She hadn't let me help her and she had ended up dead.

"I told you that you wouldn't believe me," Scary Mary said, clearly disgusted.

"Oh, I believe you," I said. "The aliens you are seeing have large heads, big eyes, and are gray. Right?"

"Yes, yes," she said, jumping a little in the booth in excitement and almost knocking over her milkshake with the large extensions on her chest.

I sighed again. "Those aren't aliens. Those are creatures

called Silicon Suckers. And my bet is they are after your breasts."

Both her hands went to cover a few inches of the mass on her chest, her eyes wide, her mouth open.

Silicon Suckers are the reason the UFO nuts think there are aliens visiting earth. They have big oblong heads with long thin excuses for chins. Their bodies are thin, humanoid, but all gray in color. Their feet are huge and they walk like they are floating through the air without a sound. And they have lived in their caves in the deserts for far longer than there have been humans around.

What drives me nuts about them are their huge eyes. They don't seem to blink, and that can just unnerve a guy, even me, a superhero.

They have no smell, but can suck moisture out of an area faster than a hundred dehumidifiers on full blast. And for some stupid reason, of all the people and superheroes and gods that exist, I am the one who has become the go-to-guy for dealing with the Silicon Suckers.

I keep wanting to tell people I play poker for a living, I work for Stan, the God of Poker, and I do my best work in casinos helping people who come into poker rooms solve their problems. As far as I know, Silicon Suckers don't even know what poker is.

Now here I was again, talking to a woman who needed help with the Silicon Suckers. If this trend didn't stop, I might start being called Silicon Sucker Boy. And I would hate that.

"So what have they been doing?" I asked, dreading the answer.

She still had her hands firmly planted over small areas of her massive breasts.

"What do you mean they might be after my breasts?"

"First tell me what they are doing," I said, sending as much Calming Power as I could generate her way. I wasn't in that good of control of that superpower yet, but by simply trying to calm a person, I sometimes could.

She took a deep breath and then nodded. "I first saw them in the parking garage off my apartment, out near the airport. They just stood there, staring at me."

"Two of them?"

"Yeah," she said. "At first I figured them for nutcases from a convention, but they are very skinny and I couldn't see costumes.

"You've seen them more times?"

She nodded. "A couple of dozen times and twice they got into my apartment. Made the place so dry I was afraid it was going to burst into flames."

"Silicon Suckers live under the desert and take moisture out of the air," I said, nodding. "Have they tried to touch you?"

"No," she said, shaking her head and shivering.

I stared into her worried eyes and knew I was way out of my depth. Any question I might have next about changes to her chest would sound bad coming from me. I needed some help.

"Hold on just a minute, would you?" I asked. "I want to call a friend to make sure there haven't been any other sightings lately."

She nodded and I motioned for Madge to come over as I stood.

"You interested in a hamburger?" I asked Scary Mary. "On me."

She nodded and I turned to Madge who had heard me. "My normal burger, one for Mary, and a shake and burger for Patty as well. I'll be right back."

Madge nodded. She would entertain Scary Mary until I got back with Patty. With luck, it would only be a minute.

CHAPTER TWO

I stepped outside the door into the warm fall day, then jumped to a spot in front of the MGM Grand main hotel lobby check-in desk. Then, before a camera could pick up my sudden appearance, I pulled myself and Patty out of the flow of time.

I loved being able to teleport, and even more being able to stop time. Actually, I couldn't stop time but it looked like I could. I actually just could step between moments in time. And I could take others with me into that moment, which made everyone else look frozen around me.

My girlfriend, Patty Ledgerwood, aka Front Desk Girl, had just finishing checking in a woman with two kids. The woman and the two kids were frozen in place moving away from the counter and Patty was smiling at me.

"Thank you," she said. "I needed a break."

"My pleasure," I said, smiling back. Just seeing Patty always made me smile. She had long brown hair that she had tied back while working. Her wonderful brown eyes were deep enough for me to get lost in and I had many, many times. Today she had on a white blouse and black slacks and a light tan MGM jacket that was the uniform of the day. She looked good in anything, but I was in love with her, so my opinion was clearly not one anyone could trust.

"So what's happening?"

"I need some help with a woman who's being visited by Silicon Suckers," I said.

"Oh, oh," Patty said. "Does she...?"

"Bigger than I thought possible," I said, indicating how large Scary Mary's breasts were.

"And you want me to help you question her about them?"

"I screwed this up once," I said. "I'd kind of like to get it right if her breasts are the problem."

Patty knew about my old girlfriend and how she had refused to give back her breast implants made out of silicon from a sacred Silicon Sucker's burial ground. The Silicon Suckers had eventually removed the breasts through her ass, for some reason the only way they know of to get inside a human body, and it had killed her.

Failing to save her always felt like one of my biggest mistakes.

Patty nodded. "Meet me in the hallway down near my car. I'll be right there."

I nodded and jumped to that spot while also stepping back into the flow of time. In Vegas a person couldn't just jump around through space without also being careful to not be picked up on cameras. Patty and I had a regular camera dead spot.

It took Patty exactly four minutes to get off work and meet me. Her boss at the MGM Grand knew what she did and that sometimes she just needed some time away. In fact, her boss was another superhero working the same area.

I jumped us out of there the moment Patty hit the camera safe area and back to a spot just in front of The Diner.

I led the way inside, telling Patty what I had ordered her. Madge was just heading back to the kitchen and Scary Mary was sitting nervously in the booth twisting the straw in her milkshake. Clearly Madge had stood and talked with her for a few minutes while I was gone.

I introduced Patty to Scary Mary and then said, "Patty knows all about the Silicon Suckers."

Patty nodded as Scary Mary sort of beamed behind all the make-up.

"I've seen them a number of times," Patty said. "And even been down in one of the caves they call sand castles."

"Wow," Scary Mary said. "I thought for sure I was going insane."

"Far from it," Patty said. "But these creatures are very dangerous, and we need to try to figure out what changed for you that started them visiting you."

"That way we have a chance of stopping them," I said.

Scary Mary nodded and I hit her again with another wave of my Relax and Trust-Me super power. She seemed to calm a little more.

Patty, who was sitting beside me in the booth, patted my leg and then leaned toward Scary Mary. "So what day exactly did you first see the Silicon Suckers?"

Scary Mary twisted her face and layered make-up around, clearly trying to think, then said, "May sixteenth."

"So, anything major happen the week before that?" Patty asked. "Anything change?"

"I got a new job," Scary Mary said without hesitation. "Five days before. I remember because it was May Eleventh, one year from the day exactly that I had my sex change operation, and I figured that was a good sign."

So Scary Mary used to be Scary Martin, but I doubted that was going to have anything to do with this case. Patty clearly didn't either because she said nothing. Again, this was Vegas. We had seen most everything.

"What was your new job?" Patty asked.

"Dispatcher," she said. "Desert High Sand and Gravel. I used to drive a truck, but after my operation Ben, the owner, said that once I got recovered, he'd find a place for me. And he did."

"What happened to the previous dispatcher?" I asked, afraid of the answer.

"Sharon? She vanished one day," Scary Mary said. "No sign of her but her ex-husband was knocking her around at one point so they're looking at him."

Patty sighed and looked down.

I would bet anything that the previous dispatcher had been killed by the Silicon Suckers. But it would never be proved. Somewhere, at some point, the trucks that Scary Mary was sending out were doing something to anger the Silicon Suckers. And since she sent them out, they were blaming her. And clearly they'd blamed the woman who had her job ahead of her.

Then Patty asked a question I hadn't thought of to ask.

"Did any other dispatchers disappear besides Sharon?"

"Joyce," Scary Mary said. "And there might have been another, but I'm not sure."

Then, suddenly she realized where we were going. "You don't think that these aliens caused them to vanish?"

Both Patty and I nodded and Scary Mary turned white under all the make-up.

Chapter Three

Madge brought the food at that point, and it gave me a chance to think. My entire premise that the Silicon Suckers were after Scary Mary's breasts had gone out the window. Most of the time I dealt with the Silicon Suckers because of land problems. They were very, very protective of their land, and had negotiated with the Gods, including Lady Luck herself, a compromise that allowed humans to build Las Vegas. But with the recent expansion, there had been many dust-ups lately over land.

This was looking like another one of those. And clearly the Silicon Suckers were warning each dispatcher in their own way, giving them time to stop, then killing them when they didn't and starting over with a new dispatcher.

Scary Mary had had no idea her job was so deadly when she took it.

After Madge put down the wonderful-smelling hamburgers and fries and left, I started to quiz Scary Mary about the business as we ate.

Turns out the company only had one large sand quarry in the desert outside of town. And the first mile of road from the pit were gravel across desert as well.

Scary Mary's job was to dispatch the trucks full of gravel or sand from the quarry to different jobs around the city or concrete mixing plants. She had to keep track of forty trucks, but in the boom times the dispatcher had managed over a hundred and had them on the go constantly for two shifts a day. She said she used to drive one of those trucks.

"I need maps of the quarry and the road in and out of it," I said. "And then I'll compare them to Silicon Sucker lands."

I took a big bite of my hamburger, then stood. "It won't take long," I said.

I headed out the door, and the moment I was on the sidewalk and the young couple walking toward Freemont Street had their back turned, I shouted to the air, "Stan. Need help in your office."

Since I didn't have an office and I didn't want Scary Mary to know what I could really do, I figured Stan's office would be as good as any.

A moment later I found myself in a standard business office and Stan in his normal black slacks and tan shirt stood facing me beside an oak desk with a computer and chair. A couple plants filled the corners and the windows looked out over Vegas from high in the air. Far higher than any office building.

"I got to teach you how to build yourself an office when you need it," he said, shaking his head.

"I can do this?" I asked, stunned, looking around at the furniture and the fantastic view of the invisible floating office. I had always figured that only the Gods could build offices.

Stan just shook his head in slight disgust and then said, "What do you need?"

I told him which maps I needed and a moment later they appeared in the air, the map of the Silicon Sucker lands floating on one side, the map of the quarry and road on the other.

"You going to tell me why you need these two maps?" he asked.

"Just put them at the same scale and overlay them," I said. "We just might see why."

He did, the two maps floating until they merged. The quarry was a long ways from the Silicon Sucker land, but the road was another matter.

"There," I said, pointing to one area where the road seemed to touch the Silicon Sucker's land. "Can you make that larger?"

The road clearly had been laid out to go around a corner of the Silicon Sucker's land, making a ninety-degree corner.

I was betting that corner had been cut off. And people had been dying because of it.

I glanced around. "Can you put us and this office right over that corner?"

An instant later we were over the corner of the dirt road, floating in the air still inside the office, only now part of the office floor under our feet was invisible.

That felt kind of creepy and cool at the same time. I really needed to learn how to do all this.

Below, I could still see the old road, but clearly a new one had been constructed a few years back that cut directly across Silicon Sucker land. More than likely the owner just figured it was desert land and no one would care. As we watched, floating invisible in an air-conditioned office above, a truck full of gravel powered through the corner leaving a trail of dust.

"Oh, shit," Stan said.

"The Suckers have been warning and then killing the truck dispatchers," I said. "Blaming them for sending the trucks across their lands. The newest one came to me because she thought she was seeing aliens."

"It was worse," Stan said.

Then something on the old road caught my eye and I could feel my stomach drop. I wished I hadn't had that bite of hamburger.

"Hang on," I said and teleported to the old section of road.

The heat of the desert hit me hard and it was a moderately cool day in the fall. I couldn't imagine how hot it was out here in the summer.

Right square in the middle of the road was a long mound of sand built crosswise to the road. Beside that were two others.

"Oh, don't tell me," Stan said, appearing beside me.

I eased over and carefully moved a little sand on one pile with my shoe, just enough to uncover the mummified remains of a human hand, drained of all moisture.

"Shit!" Stan said.

All I wanted to do was be sick. I stepped back and tried to take a deep breath of the hot air, but that didn't help much.

CHAPTER FOUR

"Where is the woman you are helping now?" Stan asked, also still staring at the three mounds clearly covering three bodies. He was the God of Poker and been around for thousands of years. And I was a superhero. That didn't mean that we had gotten used to things like this. You could never get used to this kind of thing. Ever.

"She's with Patty and Madge at The Diner," I said.

"Let's go there and figure this out," Stan said.

"Scary Mary doesn't know who we are or what we can do," I said.

Stan shook his head. "She's going to know now."

We jumped back to the booth and Scary Mary jumped so hard against the back of the booth, her large breasts just about hit her in the forehead.

Patty looked shocked as I slid in beside her and took a long drink from a glass of water. Stan pulled up a chair and took another glass of water and drank it.

Then he reached across the table and extended his hand. "I'm Stan."

"Mary," she said, taking his hand carefully. "People call me Scary Mary. And how did you do that?"

"There's a reason you came to us for help," Stan said. "Just trust us."

She nodded and said nothing, but I could tell she wanted to bolt for the door. Seeing aliens was one thing, seeing two men appear out of thin air was another.

"This has to be bad," Patty said, "or you wouldn't have come in like that."

"Very bad," I said. Then with Madge listening, I explained about the corner and what we had found on the old unused part of the road.

Mary now looked like she would be sick. "I drove for two of them," she said. "How is this possible?"

"Silicon Suckers are very, very protective of their land," I said. "They consider what they have been doing with you a warning to stop sending trucks over their land. They must have done the same thing with the other three."

"But you said they might be after my breasts," Scary Mary said.

"My first assumption; I was wrong," I said. "I had an old friend who ended up with silicon breast enhancements that were made from a sacred Silicon Sucker burial ground.

She wouldn't give them back, so the Silicon Suckers took them."

"But the issue this time is the road and that shortcut," Stan said. "You said you used to drive for this company?"

"Before my operation," Scary Mary said. "A bunch of drivers built the shortcut across that corner back in the boom times, when we were all in such a hurry to do as many loads as possible. God, such a stupid thing to kill three women over."

"Not to the Silicon Suckers," Patty said. "All their land is very sacred."

"Poker Boy," Stan said, "you deal with the Silicon Suckers more than anyone. Any idea what we need to do now?"

I honestly had no idea. There were three bodies on the old road that the police were going to need to do something with. And more than likely that would be a crime scene for some time. If the trucks kept using that shortcut, Scary Mary wouldn't live very long.

I turned to Scary Mary who was looking shocked and puzzled, or at least that's how I thought she was looking under the layers of make-up. Clearly sex-change operations didn't come with lessons in make-up.

"Is there another way in and out of that quarry?"

"South toward the freeway and then into town past the airport," she said.

"That's directly away from Silicon Sucker land," Stan said, nodding. "I'll get the police on the bodies and work with Laverne to talk with the Gods of Land Use to get permission to use the road past the Silicon Sucker lands revoked."

I nodded. Stan would take care of the surface problems. My problem still sat across from me.

"Good luck," he said. Then with a nod to Scary Mary, he vanished.

"How...how...how...?"

Scary Mary just kept staring at where he had been.

I tried one of my French Fries, but it just no longer tasted good. Somehow I still had to figure out a way to save Scary Mary's life. We would get the trucks stopped, but I had a hunch Scary Mary had insulted the Silicon Suckers for just too long a time. She would need to apologize or end up dead.

Finally Scary Mary moved her attention from the vanishing Stan to the quiet that rested over the table. She looked at Patty, then at me. "I'm still in danger, aren't I?"

Patty nodded. "I'm afraid so. But give us a little time. We'll protect you until we can get something figured out."

"Think fast," Madge said as two Silicon Suckers appeared near the door and the air in the restaurant got suddenly very, very dry.

CHAPTER FIVE

I didn't know they could teleport. That explained a great deal.

I stood and stepped toward the two alien-looking creatures. Then in their language of clicks and snaps and grunts, I said, "It is an honor to be in the presence of such great beings."

"Thank you, Poker Boy," the one on the right said in clear English without seeming to move his lips. "The honor is ours. Today you visited the great scar in our lands."

"Yes, I did not know about it until today," I said, having no idea what to say but the truth. "I have become very upset at such an insult to my wonderful friends, the Silicon Suckers. The human vehicles that crossed across your sacred lands and damaged them are being stopped and will not come near your lands again. The humans must retrieve the dead that caused such damage, but then that path near your sacred lands will be closed completely."

The restaurant was becoming tinder dry and Patty and Scary Mary sat perfectly still in the booth. Madge stood near her counter, also not moving.

"When will this ceremony take place?" the Silicon Sucker asked.

I had no idea what he meant by ceremony, but with that corner being a crime scene, we wouldn't be able to do anything there anytime soon. I bowed slightly. "May we beg for one half of a moon cycle to prepare and for the humans to finish removing their dead?"

The Silicon Sucker bowed slightly, then said, "Yes, that will be acceptable."

I had just bought us and Scary Mary two weeks. I hoped that would be enough time.

Then the Silicon Sucker turned and looked at Scary Mary for a moment, then back at me. If they stepped toward her, there would be nothing I could do to stop them that wouldn't insult them deeply and maybe cause a war between the Gods and Silicon Suckers. So far, in my understanding, there had only been two such wars throughout all time. Both fought over land.

Scary Mary had damaged their land in their minds. No God or Superhero could or would stop them if they wanted to take her.

"Will the human that sent such machines over our land be at the ceremony?"

"She did not understand what she was doing until she received your warnings and came to me. She is disgusted at her carelessness, and is the reason it is stopping now. She will bow in great respect and offer herself and her gifts in hopes the great Silicon Suckers will allow her to live."

He bowed slightly again and then said, "We will be watching."

"It was an honor as always," I said, bowing to them.

Both bowed in return and then vanished.

"Open the door and let some moisture in here," Madge said after a moment.

I did as I was told and then went back to the booth and drank three glasses of the water that Madge brought.

We had two weeks to save Scary Mary's life.

CHAPTER SIX

We failed.

That afternoon at The Diner we tried our best to convince Scary Mary to keep her mouth shut about the murders and what she knew. And never say anything about the Silicon Suckers, but it ended up under questioning she didn't remain quiet.

Or couldn't. I never knew.

The murders hit the headlines, of course. When it became known that the corpses had been hollowed out, with most of the insides pulled out of the victims' asses, it got even more sensational. The press called them the "Empty Mummy Murders."

I didn't want to mention to the press that most mummies were empty.

After the police were done, Stan got the Gods of Land

Use to go in and close off and destroy any sign of any road across the Silicon Suckers land, and even had them replant new desert grass and weeds.

Two major rocks were placed at both ends of the old shortcut to make sure no one went out there over the Silicon Sucker land.

And, of course, the road to the crime scene was closed off completely from the quarry to the location of the bodies and also from the highway to the location at the corner.

But Scary Mary just couldn't keep her mouth shut. She started insisting that it was aliens who had killed the women. And that there were people in The Diner who could appear and disappear.

That sounded totally insane, so the police started investigating her past and her sanity and came up will all sorts of things that didn't look good besides her make-up.

Scary Mary was tossed into custody not only as a suspect in the murders, but also for other events that happened in her past, including the accidental drowning in a pool of Scary Mary's first wife when Scary Mary was a he.

Her picture in all its strange made-up glory hit the front page of the newspaper as a primary suspect in the Empty Mummy Murders.

So on the day of the ceremony, Scary Mary could not attend.

I wanted to jump into jail and spring her for the ceremony, but Stan wouldn't let me. He said we didn't do things that way.

I did the best I could in the ceremony, leaving offerings of five thermoses of hot chocolate at each end of the now repaired scar in the land. Silicon Suckers treasured hot chocolate as a sacred drug that allowed them to produce more Silicon Suckers. I figured five at each end would show them how serious I thought the scar was.

Denton, the God of Land Use Planning, who was the God who had originally negotiated the settlement of lands around Las Vegas, appeared and begged for the forgiveness of the great beings.

There just wasn't much else we could do.

No Silicon Suckers showed up, so we left the thermoses sitting in the sand in the desert.

Four days later Scary Mary vanished from her holding cell. Her body was found where the others had been found two days earlier. All her organs had all been cleaned out through her ass and her skin was mumified.

Scary Mary became the fourth known victim of the Empty Mummy Murderer. Of course, the case was never solved.

I was batting zero-for-two. Two women had come to me for help with the Silicon Suckers and both had been killed. I moped around for a few days until finally Patty got fed up with me and went with me to talk with Stan.

We ended up in another floating office far over the city. The view was stunning, but I noticed Stan had his windows turned so that he couldn't see in the direction of the quarry.

He was sitting behind a big oak desk with nothing on it. Patty and I dropped down onto the leather couch.

With Patty pushing me on, I mentioned what was bothering me to Stan.

He just shrugged. "Nothing you could do when a person won't help themselves and just keep their mouth shut."

"I mentioned that a few times as well," Patty said, shaking her head. "But he's determined to feel bad."

"It feels like crap," I said. "Even though I couldn't do anything."

"Yeah, it does," Stan said. "But do you win every hand you play at a poker table?"

"Of course not," I said, almost angry that he had suggested that. "But when I lose a hand there I don't have someone die."

"True," Stan said, "but you win a hell of a lot more than you lose in the saving-people game. And that's the key to remember."

"Yeah," Laverne said, suddenly appearing standing beside Stan behind his desk, "remember the ones you saved."

Patty and I both jumped to our feet, because when Lady Luck appears, you don't sit there slouching on the couch.

Lady Luck went on. "Remember you and your team saved me once. And the entire human race another time. And you've even saved a few people from the Silicon Suckers over the last few years, which is more than most have done."

All I could do was nod. She was right.

"So get over it and get back to work," she said, smiling at me.

When Lady Luck smiles at you, trust me, you can feel it. And I did. I felt a ton better, and was suddenly back thinking again instead of just feeling sorry for myself for losing Scary Mary.

"Stan," Lady Luck said, "teach Poker Boy how to build himself an office, would you? It's about time he and his team have one of their own, don't you think?"

Then she vanished.

Stan laughed and stood from behind his desk. "That's the first time I have ever heard her give a pep talk."

"You're kidding?" I asked, feeling stunned.

"Three thousand years, never seen it happen."

Suddenly even more of the weight seemed to lift from my shoulders.

Patty gave me a hug and then a big, long kiss.

"Hey, not in my office," Stan said.

I broke away from Patty just long enough to say, "Then teach me how to build one of my own." Then I went back to kissing Patty.

"Nag, nag, nag," Stan said.

Fighting the Fuzzy Wuzzy

Chapter One

I first met Wolfgang Sucker two nights before the great Fuzzy-Wuzzy war.

Now, as Poker Boy, I meet my share of strange beings, mostly just people sitting around poker tables as I try to earn enough to get to the next place where I have to do my superhero thing and rescue someone or fight the bad guy. (And sometimes along the way I even save a dog or two, but that's not part of my job description. It just sort of happens.)

But Wolfgang Sucker was one of the stranger people who ever walked up to me and asked for help.

Honestly, I didn't see him until he was standing in front of me. I was standing against one of the large stone columns in the main lobby of the MGM Grand Hotel and Casino on the Strip in Las Vegas. My girlfriend and sidekick, Patty Ledgerwood, aka Front Desk Girl, had a couple of things to finish before she got off work and we headed back to her place.

I have no idea how Wolfgang Sucker knew who I was, and I sure didn't notice him until he was standing in front of me.

"Poker Boy?" he asked, his voice sounding like someone sanding a piece of furniture. "I need your help if you don't mind. My name is Wolfgang Sucker."

Actually, what he really needed was a couple bottles of Scope and a bath. His breath smelled like he had bathed in onions, but I didn't say anything. Not my place to judge people who are asking for my help.

That was the exact moment, as the crowds of people moved around and past us in the huge lobby, talking and laughing, that I actually focused on Wolfgang Sucker for the first time.

And actually saw him, in all of his blueness.

Not kidding. He was blue, skin and all, and there was a lot of skin showing. He only wore a pair of tight pants that seemed more like skin than pants, showing parts that no man should show in public without getting arrested.

If the blue had been painted on I would have thought him to be a refugee from the Blue Man Group that performed all the time in Vegas. But his skin was a real blue.

He had on no shirt at all, but security in the MGM Grand didn't seem to even notice. In fact no one seemed to notice.

He stood about six inches taller than my six-foot frame and weighed far under my weight, which gave Wolfgang the look of a tall stick with arms. I had seen skinnier people, but not many. Skinnier people were usually high school basketball players, and Wolfgang looked to be a ways from high school age, even though his skin was as blue and smooth as it comes.

Besides being blue, what made Wolfgang really stand out was his nervous tick of constantly turning his head from side to side, not fast, but slowly, like a lighthouse beacon moving around.

He seldom looked at anyone directly with his deep blue eyes. His gaze just sort of passed over you until his head was completely sideways to you, then it slowly came back the other direction.

After about two minutes of talking with him that first time, I wanted to just grab his head and hold it still, but I was afraid his body would start rotating under it. And I didn't want to get that close to that breath, either.

But worse yet, if that and the bad breath wasn't bad enough, his head was completely bald and covered in white tattoo patterns of some weird alien design that looked at first a little like a giant net with a squid in the middle. But every time he turned his head and then started back, the tattoos seemed to shift without really shifting so that by the time his head was turned one hundred and eighty degrees in the other direction, the scars gave a different image.

And they moved around, all over his face, his head, down his neck.

Never once did the image repeat that I could tell.

I have no idea how the tattoos changed, but I sure watched them a lot trying to figure it out since there was no point trying to look the guy in the eyes. At one point I actually thought about fighting my way upstream into the onions to get closer to see how those marks were shifting like that. But I didn't.

After a moment or two of staring at Wolfgang Sucker's head, I realized he had been talking about something, but his rasping voice was so low I couldn't hear it over the loud sounds of the huge lobby and the casino down the hallway.

I held up my hand for him to stop. "We're going to need to get to a place where we can talk in a little more quiet. I'm having trouble hearing you. Can you hold on for less than one minute?"

I could see Patty heading toward us across the lobby, and I most certainly wanted her to hear what kind of help this guy needed from me. And I wanted her to meet him, otherwise she would just never believe me.

As she approached, Wolfgang Sucker turned and bowed just slightly at the waist. "Front Desk Girl. Good, I was also hoping you might help as well."

Patty's eyes got round and she glanced at me before going back to staring at Wolfgang Sucker as he introduced himself.

I just shrugged and indicated I didn't know what the guy wanted.

It was a nice, comfortable October night outside, so I figured there would be less noise out through the front doors than in the lobby, so I indicated we should all move that way.

He wouldn't budge. "No," he said firmly. "The Fuzzy-

Wuzzys are going to be arriving out there, near the front door."

Now Patty's eyes really got large, and I'm sure I had the worst puzzled look on my face. It was then that it occurred to me that this might be some practical joke, played on us by one of the gambling gods.

In fact, the more I thought about, the more I was sure it was a joke. The only "Fuzzy-Wuzzy" I knew came from an old children's rhyme about a bald bear or something like that.

I slipped Patty and I out of time, leaving old Wolfgang frozen with the rest of the lobby.

I always got a kick out of doing that. It was a real power, compared to some of my other powers like getting someone to believe me or reading their faces to see if they were telling the truth. Slipping into a moment in time was just fun and cool. I couldn't hold it very long, not more than a few minutes, but each time I did it, I got stronger. And since all my power came from casinos, it was pretty easy to do while standing inside one of the bigger ones on the planet.

"Is this guy for real?" Patty asked, staring at the scars on his head that were now frozen in the moment into a picture of some sort of alien cow being eaten by some other creature with fangs.

"I have no idea," I said. "I'm guessing it's a joke someone's pulling on us. It finally dawned on me that with a name like Wolfgang Sucker, we might be the real suckers. And it was the Fuzzy-Wuzzy part that convinced me."

Patty nodded, so I shouted into the air, "Stan!"

An instant later Stan appeared beside us. It only took him a second to notice Wolfgang and start staring, his mouth open.

"So what's the joke?" I asked.

Stan didn't answer, just sort of walked around Wolfgang, then came back to me.

"No joke," Stan said. "This guy is a Searchlight. I've only seen one and that was a number of centuries back."

"Searchlight?" Patty asked.

"Yeah, the name we call them, more than likely because of that annoying head movement they do. There are only a few thousand of them and they live forever, or so the myths say. No one knows where they came from, where they live, or what they even do. Or what those changing pictures on their heads mean."

"You're serious?" I asked, still thinking this was an elaborate joke that Stan was part of.

"Completely," Stan said, still staring at Wolfgang. "Did he say what he wanted?"

"My help is all I managed to hear because he talks so softly."

Stan frowned. "Not good, really not good."

"And he wanted me to help as well," Patty said. "And he knew who I was."

Okay, maybe this wasn't a joke. I sure didn't like the sound of the God of Poker saying "Not good, really not good." In all the years I had worked as a superhero for him, he had never said anything like that. Even joking.

"He wouldn't go outside to talk because he said the Fuzzy-Wuzzys were going to be out there, or something like that."

"Oh, shit," Stan said, his normally calm face now almost pale.

Having the God of Poker looked scared about a guy named after a hairless bear didn't make me feel any better about this situation either. I had no idea what the problem even was and I was starting to panic.

Stan turned to Patty. "Get our guest to a meeting room. I'll be back with Laverne and some other help as soon as I can. And you had better call in your team."

At that Stan vanished.

"Seems our nice evening at your place has just been postponed," I said.

All Patty could do was nod as I stuck us back into real time and let the noise of the crowd wash back over us like a pounding wave. Being in the silence of between-time was always nice.

Patty indicated that Wolfgang Sucker should follow her. "I have a meeting room we can talk in."

"Have you contacted Laverne and the others?" Wolfgang asked in his raspy voice, barely loud enough for me to hear.

"We have," I said. "They'll join us in the meeting room."

He said simply, "Good. We will need everyone if we are to survive this coming battle."

I stared at him as we walked, not liking the sound of that

either. And if he wanted to contact Laverne, why didn't he just go to her?

And then he said, just loud enough for me to hear, "And we are called Searchlights because we stand guard over humanity, always watching for trouble, not because of our head movement."

I walked a few steps with my mouth open. Even with Patty and I out of time, he had overheard what we had said.

That was creepy, just creepy.

Chapter Two

The meeting room that Patty led us to was off the main corridor leading to the casino from the lobby, and it could hold fifty people, if needed. It was the standard business meeting room that you saw everywhere in every hotel. Only this one had the bright MGM Grand Hotel colors and logo on the carpet and a huge polished wooden table in the middle of the room with about thirty leather chairs around it.

When Patty closed the door, the sounds from outside shut off as if someone had thrown a switch. I had no doubt that in this place I would be able to actually hear Wolfgang speak clearly in his rasping voice, but he didn't say anything and I had no idea what to ask him.

I was still trying to get over the fact that he could hear us between moments in time.

He moved with gliding steps to the head of the table and stood behind the leather chair there and said nothing. His head just kept shifting from side to side, slowly.

Patty jumped on her cell phone and called both Screamer and The Smoke and told them where we were.

"They are both about ten minutes away," Pati said.

"Good," I said. I didn't say that I wish I knew what we were up against so I could tell them what was going on.

A moment later Stan, the God of Poker appeared with Burt, the God of Casino Operations, and Laverne, Lady Luck herself. Laverne was dressed in a black pants suit.

Now I knew for sure this was no joke.

Stan and Burt just looked worried.

"Wolfgang," she said, moving toward our guest. "It is always a pleasure to see you again.

Then Lady Luck bowed slightly in a show of respect, which flat stunned me. Laverne was one of the most powerful gods there was in all the deities. She didn't bow to anyone I knew of.

At least until now.

Wolfgang bowed slightly in the same way to Laverne as he had done to Patty. "It is also good to see you," he said, his voice clear even though it sounded more like someone was taking sandpaper to the large wooden meeting table in the room.

Laverne got right to the point. "Am I to understand that the Fuzzy-Wuzzys are coming back?"

"They are," Wolfgang said, his head never stopping for an instant.

"How long until they reach this plane of existence?" Laverne asked.

"They will become clear to you in five hours, and to the rest of the human race in two days; just under forty-nine of your hours. If they cannot be stopped before that point, I fear for the human race."

I glanced at my watch. It was just past eleven in the evening. So they would appear to humans in two days at midnight. Whatever they were. And Laverne would be able to see them coming in five hours.

And I assumed something called a Fuzzy-Wuzzy appearing suddenly to humans was a bad thing from the way everyone was acting and talking. But at this point I didn't have a clue why or how we were all going to die.

And I also didn't know where they were appearing from exactly. Laverne and Wolfgang sure seemed to think all this was serious. For the moment, since Laverne was the big boss, that was good enough for me.

"Are there other Searchlights involved?" Laverne asked.

"We all are," Wolfgang Sucker said. "At the moment they are contacting all the other deities, and a delegation has been sent to the Fates. We have little time."

Now I really wanted to know why this guy came to me first.

Laverne nodded. "I assume this is a worldwide attack this time?"

"It is," Wolfgang said. "They are stronger and are coming in more numbers than before. They will not be easily tricked or defeated this time."

"Humanity barely survived the last time," Laverne said, shaking her head.

Now that didn't sound good at all.

Patty took my hand and squeezed it.

"And why are you here?" Laverne asked. "Is this an attack point?"

"Yes, they are opening a portal just in front of this building. One of a thousand such portals around the world."

"A thousand?" Laverne asked softly, more to herself than to Wolfgang.

He said nothing.

Laverne again bowed slightly to Wolfgang Sucker. "Thank you and your people for the warning and the help in this coming fight. As always, it is appreciated."

"Unless I am needed before, I will come back to this room in twelve hours," he said, returning the bow.

Then he vanished.

"Damn," Laverne said, turning to the rest of us shaking her head. "I worried about this day coming again. I just hoped it never would."

Now the silence in the large meeting room felt like a huge weight just pressing down on everything.

"Stan," Laverne said, "please explain to Poker Boy and his team what's happening."

Then she and Burt vanished.

Stan moved over to the table and sat down hard.

Seeing the God of Poker completely shaken and hearing Lady Luck herself actually swear wasn't a good sign.

Not good at all.

Chapter Three

Patty and I went around the big table and sat facing Stan. Patty kept her hand in mine and I liked that. Together we were a lot stronger than we were apart. And from the sounds of whatever we were fighting, we were going to need all the strength we could muster.

I wanted to ask Stan about a thousand questions starting off with why something that could destroy mankind was called a "Fuzzy-Wuzzy" and why, if this Searchlight guy wanted to talk to Laverne, did he come to me first, but I decided to just wait. It sounded like these blue guys were a lot older than some silly children's rhyme and more than likely had some ritual they had to follow.

Both Screamer and The Smoke came through the door two minutes later, for a moment letting in the loud sounds from the hallway and casino before closing the door.

Screamer was a superhero as well and his main power was the ability to connect minds of people and put images in people's heads. He got his name from a time when the police asked him to get the location of a buried-alive woman from a killer's mind. He made the guy scream and the nickname stuck.

The Smoke is a superhero working for the animal deities. He's actually a werewolf of sorts, with complete control of which form he is in, and he can go through walls with ease. That's a nifty trick that has come in handy a few times since he became part of our team.

"So what are we in for this time?" Screamer asked dropping into one of the soft leather chairs and smiling.

Then he noticed that Patty and I and Stan were all looking very upset.

"I fear this is no good," The Smoke said, moving around and standing off to my right near the wall. The Smoke liked to stand, and only sat when he needed to.

Stan nodded and took a deep breath. "It's bad and everyone is working on this. The Fuzzy-Wuzzys are coming back."

"Oh, no," The Smoke said, coming over and also dropping into a chair beside me.

It seemed clear that he knew what the Fuzzy-Wuzzys were. Screamer just looked as puzzled as I felt.

"Okay," I said to Stan. "Time to tell us what these things are."

"History first. Do you know the story of the continent of Atlantis?"

"Was that a real place?" Patty asked a fraction of a moment before I did.

"It was the home of most humans on the planet at the time," Stan said. "A wonderful place, very beautiful. It was mankind's third home on this planet, and it was destroyed in the first Fuzzy-Wuzzy invasion."

I desperately wanted to ask him what the first two homes were and where they were and how old was he, but I managed to stay on topic somehow. At this point I had so many questions there was no chance I was going to remember them all.

"How did they destroy Atlantis?" Patty asked.

"They didn't, we did," Stan said. "We sank it to kill them and drive them back."

I could hear a pin drop in that huge meeting room at that moment. Stan seemed very far away and didn't want to meet my gaze at all.

"You sank it?"

He nodded. "All the gods combined, along with the Fates and help from the Searchlights. We all sank it. We killed almost a billion humans to save everyone else. Humanity almost didn't recover."

Again the silence filled the room, and my stomach felt like it was going to crawl up through my throat and lodge in my nose. I just couldn't think of one damn thing to say.

Patty squeezed my hand really, really hard.

"Why are these Fuzzy-Wuzzy things so bad?" Screamer finally asked.

"Humans are a giant buffet to them," Stan said. "They eat everything except bones and fingernails and hair."

"They also eat most animals," The Smoke said. "And trees and brush and everything."

"Where do they come from?" Patty asked.

"They are coming from the alternation dimension over down the time stream," Stan said.

I felt like a kid in school and the teacher was talking, but nothing was making sense. "Do you want to try to explain that?" I asked, "or for now can we just say they come from another dimension?"

Stan nodded. "Just say another parallel dimension, only the humans in all the dimensions in that direction along the time stream lost the war to the Fuzzy-Wuzzys and are gone. We are their next meal. But we managed to stop them so soundly last time that it has taken them thousands of years to recover."

Again the silence.

"So what do these things look like?" I asked. "Why the name Fuzzy-Wuzzy? And why can't we get the armies of the world to pitch into this fight?"

Stan pointed to the nail on his little finger. "They are bugs, covered in a light fur, and over a hundred of them could fit on my little fingernail."

I just stared at him. "You are telling me this great threat to humanity is a mass invasion of tiny, tiny, furry bed bugs?"

He nodded. "They can take a human body down to a pile of bones and Fuzzy-Wuzzy black shit in two seconds. And once here they can move faster than any man can run. In Atlantis I watched them mow through a crowd of thousands before the crowd knew what hit it. The more they eat and digest, the smarter they get and the harder they are to stop."

I opened my mouth and again could think of nothing to say.

"So you drowned them the last time?" Screamer finally asked.

Stan nodded. "We did, and poured an awful lot of ocean water through the dimensional portals. But they only came through five portals last time, not like the thousands they are attacking through this time."

It finally dawned on me what was bothering me.

"You are telling me these things are very, very tiny. Yet you are acting like they are intelligent. That's not possible."

"Hive mind," Stan said. "Alone or in groups of only a few thousand, they have no ability to think and can be easily killed. In fact, in groups of under a thousand they don't eat. But in masses, they are eating and thinking machines of fantastic ability and intellect. Somehow they transport the energy from eating to the hive mind. No one is sure how that works."

"So what weapons kill them?" Screamer asked. "And can anything protect a human from them?"

"Stepping on them kills them," Stan said. "Drowning, flame, anything with any force. And chemicals of all types kill them. Just like any other tiny bugs. The problem is that they move so fast and together that they can loose millions and not be bothered in the slightest."

"And protection?"

"They can't eat through anything inorganic," Stan said. "Stone, rock, rubber, things like that. But they can go through wood like it doesn't exist."

Again the intense silence.

I couldn't think of another question to ask Stan, and neither could anyone else it seemed, so Stan nodded and said, "I'll be back in an hour to see if you four have any ideas on how to fight these things."

Then he vanished.

The silence again. I was starting to really, really hate the silence.

Finally I said, "We are so screwed."

None of my team challenged me on that.

Chapter Four

After we all sat there in the silence for what seemed like the longest time, I finally couldn't take it anymore. "Anyone up for a milkshake?"

Normally we met downtown, at The Diner, to plan operations and work to save people. It just seemed natural to go there now. It wasn't more than a small hole-in-the-wall around the corner on a side street from the Horseshoe Casino. The Diner was decorated in fake 1960sstuff and had a phony jukebox playing in the background all the time.

Before anyone could say anything, Stan showed back up. "I would love a milkshake."

A moment later we all appeared in The Diner sitting at our favorite booth while Stan sat in a chair in front of the booth. Madge, our normal waitress, was sitting at the counter shaking her head. In all the years we had been coming into this little place, I had never seen Madge sit down. She was a superhero working for the Gods of Food and Beverage, and she knew about us.

Madge always had an attitude, and was the best waitress I had ever met. And when in the 1960s diner uniform, she always wore too much make-up and light slacks three sizes too tight. She was a large woman both top and bottom, and it was a standing joke that no one should be allowed to watch Madge walk away or bend over.

Since we discovered she was a superhero as well, she had become a sort of unofficial member of my team.

We were the only ones in The Diner, and it was clear the place was closed, something I had also never seen. At least the oldies station was still playing softly on the radio.

Stan shouted over to Madge. "Our regular, then come join us. We've got planning to do."

Madge glanced around and it was clear from the black streaks of thick make-up on her face that she had been crying. She must have heard about humanity's upcoming doom.

She nodded and got to her feet, using a napkin to smear the make-up even more.

"So when are you going to teach me that jumping around in space trick?" I asked Stan. I'd been bugging him about learning that now for a while, but he had just never gotten around to showing me how that power worked. He had never said I didn't have the power, only that I needed to learn how to do it.

"Next week," he said, 'if we can figure out a way to win this war, and there is a next week."

I nodded. "Deal. Now tell me why the Searchlight came to me instead of going straight to Laverne?"

"Custom," Stan said. "When you want to see the queen, you don't just barge into the throne room, you talk to her guards."

"Real old school," I said.

Stan just nodded.

From the counter the milkshake machines started up.

"So how come you are back here with us?" Patty asked.

"I'm worthless with the Gods," he said. "I told Laverne I'd do better back here with your team, and she agreed."

Over the years, our team had saved the planet a couple of times, and saved Lady Luck herself more than once. She clearly had a lot of faith in us to send Stan to help us. I just wish I had as much faith in us right now as Lady Luck did.

I was just a lowly poker-playing superhero. What could I do against an invasion of tiny bugs? I couldn't read their faces because more than likely they didn't have any. I couldn't take their money, or bluff them off their chips. And I...

"Bluff," I said out loud.

Everyone at the table looked at me.

I had zero idea what I meant by that, but my little voice, the voice that told me when to bet and when to fold, was shouting that the key to all this was bluffing. And I trusted that little voice.

But how the hell do you bluff a hive mind of millions of bugs?

"You want to explain that outburst?" Stan said.

I glanced around the booth, realizing that everyone was just staring at me. Madge was just finishing the milkshakes.

"Not sure what I meant," I said. "I need more information. Wolfgang said that they are coming through one thousand portals? How big is a portal?"

"In Atlantis a portal was about five feet around, but impossible to block."

"And we know where all these portals are going to appear?" I asked.

Stan nodded. "The Searchlights do, and the top gods will be able to see them forming in a few more hours as well."

I wish I could figure out what I was thinking. It was just there, at the back of my mind, but darned if I could figure it out.

Then I had another idea.

I took Patty's hand that had been resting on my right leg and placed it on the top of the table with my hand on top of hers. Then I looked at Screamer.

"I have an idea, but can't quite get it to form. Come on in with Patty and help me figure it out."

Screamer nodded, reached across the table, and put his hand on top of ours.

Suddenly Screamer and Patty were in my mind. We had joined minds so many times on missions over the last few years, the sensation almost felt familiar.

Weird, but familiar.

Bluff. What am I thinking about, bluffing the Fuzzy-Wuzzy?

I focused, trying to dig up the idea as Screamer and Patty searched inside my head. After what seemed like only an instant Screamer thought at me directly, *Just what the word means. To mislead.*

He's right, Patty thought at me. *You are thinking we can mislead the Fuzzy-Wuzzy.*

Screamer took his hand away and I was again alone in my own head. But I did have a part of an idea.

"Stan, do any of the gods or Fates have the ability to open one of these portals?"

"I wouldn't know why not," he said. "It's similar to the power needed to slip between a moment in time. I've never tried it since I have no desire to meet myself in another dimension."

Suddenly I was confused again.

"Are you saying that the dimension to our left has never been attacked by these things?"

"No, it would take you moving over thousands of millions of billions of dimensions to find one that was never attacked. Think of a river. Every time there is a new event, it splits off two dimensions, like two almost-identical branches of the same river. When you all saved Lady Luck from the Bookkeepers' little mistake, you created two dimensions, this one where you saved her, and one where you didn't. So since the last attack on Atlantis, billions of new timelines have formed to the left of this one."

"Every major event creates a new timeline, a new dimension?" Patty asked? "Every event? Anywhere?"

My head hurt.

"That's right," Stan said. "If we stop these things this time, there will be a new dimension where we don't stop them. And in that timeline over, those of us existing in the neighboring dimension will have to fight them. And so on. The Fuzzy-Wuzzy need to keep eating, thus their need and ability to keep moving from dimension to dimension and eating entire populations. There are a lot of dimensions out there."

"I'm really sorry I asked that question," I said.

"I am sorry you asked it as well," The Smoke said. "But we must focus on this dimension and let the others fight their own fights."

At that moment Madge brought the milkshakes. She had managed to wash her face, but still looked completely distraught.

"Any ideas?" she asked, sliding a vanilla milkshake in front of me.

"A couple," I said.

At that she brightened up. Then she turned to The Smoke. "It's going to be a minute on the hamburger. I had the grill turned off."

The Smoke's regular was a hamburger, almost rare, instead of a milkshake.

The Smoke nodded and said, "Pull up a chair."

"So what's the idea?" Stan asked.

"I need one more piece of information. When these things run out of human food, do they attack each other?"

He shrugged. "I honestly don't know. Let me find out about both questions."

He vanished, and then a moment later he and Lady Luck herself appeared back. Lady Luck sat down in Stan's chair and Stan quickly pulled over another chair.

"So what are you thinking?" Laverne asked.

I took a deep breath and stared at the most frightening god that existed, as far as I was concerned. "We need to bluff the Fuzzy-Wuzzy into going to another dimension, one where they have already eaten us all. Stan says we can form these gates to other dimensions."

"Easily," she said. "We don't as a general rule."

"Can the portals be made to be one way?" I asked. The idea was starting to form and I was getting excited.

"They can be," Laverne said, looking puzzled.

"I asked Stan if these things ever got hungry enough to eat each other," I said, "and he went to ask you."

Wolfgang Sucker appeared in all his bright blue glory, standing beside the booth next to Stan, his onion breath covering us all instantly as his head turned slowly from side-to-side.

Madge jumped up and took a couple of steps back, the look of shock on her face very clear.

"They must eat every fifty years or they will turn on each

other," Wolfgang said, his voice again like sandpaper on a hard surface. "It takes them almost a half year to form the portals."

"How long does it take us to form a portal?" I asked.

"Instantly," Laverne said.

"One more question," I said. "When they leave a dimension, do they leave anyone behind?"

"Nothing but a stripped planet with nothing alive remaining," Wolfgang said.

I smiled. This idea just might work if there wasn't something I didn't know.

"Can you form a portal to one hundred dimensions back along the line of the Fuzzy-Wuzzy conquests?"

"We can go back thousands of dimensions, but all the worlds would still be dead," the Searchlight said.

I nodded. "Okay, here's the idea. "Form a portal to one of the destroyed worlds a thousand worlds away, and put *that* portal directly over *their* portal and somehow seal the connection. You won't be blocking it. They just won't know they haven't arrived here yet."

Stan and Laverne were nodding so I went on. "That way when they come through their portal, trying to get to us, they instead end up in a dead dimension without their knowing it. We bluff them."

"Actually," Screamer asked, smiling, "why not divide them into a thousand different dead worlds over a thousand dimensions, so far back they will only be able to eat themselves?"

Laverne stared at me for a moment, her dark eyes seeming

to cut through me like I didn't exist. Then she said softly, "That might work."

At the same instant she and Stan and the Searchlight vanished.

Patty squeezed my hand and Screamer and The Smoke just smiled.

"You guys are really something," Madge said, shaking her head. "Milkshakes are on me."

I just hoped my idea worked and this wasn't going to be my last milkshake ever.

CHAPTER FIVE

Forty-eight hours later, I stood with Stan, Patty, Screamer, The Smoke, and Wolfgang Sucker in a "you can't see us" bubble around the portal forming in the driveway to the MGM Grand Hotel valet parking.

Around us, Las Vegas went on with its normal, noisy life. The night air was warm, but thankfully not hot.

I was the one holding the "can't-see-us" bubble. Up until yesterday I didn't know I had that power.

Stan, with help from the Searchlight, and with energy support from all of us, had formed a dimensional portal that fit tightly over the Fuzzy-Wuzzy's portal. Stan's portal shifted the Fuzzy-Wuzzy almost a thousand dimensions back.

From what I understood, the Fuzzy-Wuzzy could only move from one dimension to the next every half-year; so if this worked, it would take them hundreds and hundreds of years to get back. And since they would turn on each other to eat long before that, they might never make it back.

And we were splitting the entire invasion force up into a thousand parts over thousands of dead dimensions.

All over the planet right now, Searchlights and Gods were forming dimensional portals over the Fuzzy-Wuzzy portals.

It was our only plan of defense, and it had been my idea. I just hoped it worked. I hadn't slept, worrying about it.

If this plan didn't work, we were all going to be the first appetizer for a very hungry horde of bugs.

"Five, four, three," Patty said, counting down.

All of us poured energy to Stan as we had practiced, while the Searchlight held the connection between the two portals.

Since I wasn't a god, I couldn't see the forming Fuzzy-Wuzzy portal until suddenly it formed directly under the one Stan had formed.

A blur of black seemed to fill the opening of the portal. It went on and on and on.

And then nothing.

"I think they have all gone through," Stan said, beads of sweat forming on his face.

Suddenly the dimensional portal formed by the Fuzzy-Wuzzy closed and Stan slumped to the ground, breathing hard.

"I hate those bugs," he said, panting.

For a moment the Searchlight stood there, then he said,

with his rough voice loud enough to hear even against all the noise of a Las Vegas night:

"It has worked."

Then he turned to all of us as Stan climbed back to his feet.

Suddenly Wolfgang Sucker's head stopped moving, and his blue eyes stared directly at us.

"This great battle will be shown on the heads of a thousand of my brothers for centuries to come. It has been my honor to be a member of your team, Poker Boy."

With that he vanished.

"Well, you all did it again," Laverne said from directly behind me.

We all spun to face Lady Luck.

She was smiling, and when Lady Luck smiles on you, you know it.

"Someday we might have to start paying all of you if this keeps up."

She laughed at her own joke, since superheroes don't get paid.

Then she winked at Stan. "Teach him how to jump through space, would you? I worry about him taking so many airplane flights."

Then she got serious. "Thank you. Every one of you. It was a perfect bluff, and a perfect idea. I just wish you all had been around in Atlantis' time."

With that she vanished.

Stan turned to me, smiling. "Well done, as usual."

I didn't know what to say. I was so stunned that my idea had worked, I just sort of felt nothing.

"Milkshakes are on me," Stan said. Then he smiled even larger, "If you can get us there, Poker Boy, without calling a cab."

And suddenly I knew how to jump through space, from one location to another. I don't know how I knew, but I just did.

"That's a deal," I said. I took Patty's hand in mine and said to Stan, "Race you."

An instant later, I had my team sitting in our regular booth in The Diner as a fraction of a second later Stan appeared, still smiling.

Wow, that felt good.

Patty just squeezed my hand and smiled. Then she whispered in my ear, "Now we can see a lot more of each other."

I liked that idea. I liked it a lot.

The sound of crashing glass made us all turn around as one.

Madge was dancing on the counter in front of the kitchen. She seemed to be doing dance moves not thought of in years, and considering she always wore slacks three sizes too tight, it wasn't a scene that any sane person could watch for very long.

Stan started laughing and The Smoke just covered his eyes.

After a moment, all of us started laughing.

"Why not?" Screamer asked, and got up and started dancing as well, quickly joining Madge on the countertop.

"Looks like milkshakes are going to be a minute," I said between huge laughs of relief.

"Thanks to all of you," Stan said, "we have the time to wait."

Nonexistent No More

Chapter 1

Who knew that Wolfgang Sucker had a wife? A Mrs. Sucker.

And since Wolfgang was a blue-skinned Searchlight, if I had thought of him having a wife, I would have assumed that Mrs. Sucker would be blue as well.

Wrong. Mrs. Wolfgang Sucker was bright pink, and depending on the light, the pink shifted to bright purple, very bright purple. And she had wide brown eyes instead of blue eyes.

Just as the first time I saw her husband, I first saw Mrs. Sucker walking toward me across the lobby of the MGM Grand Hotel and Casino in Las Vegas. I was leaning against one of the stone pillars in the lobby waiting for my girlfriend and sidekick, Patty Ledgerwood, aka Front Desk Girl to get off work.

Stunning didn't begin to describe Mrs. Sucker, even though no one in the lobby seemed to even notice her, and they should have. Every man in the room should have been staring. Her body suit, or at least I hoped it was a body suit, blended perfectly with her pink/purple skin making her look to be a very bright nude, only with no real details showing.

Maybe she didn't have any of those details. I just didn't know. In fact, what I knew about Searchlights wasn't much, other than they were very, very powerful.

She stood as thin and as tall as her husband, at least six-six, and she couldn't have weighed more than one-hundred-and-twenty pounds.

And I was sure that most of that weight she carried on the front of her chest.

She was the wet dream of every modeling agency on the planet. Even with the bright pink/purple skin color. It was just weird how the color kept changing from shade to shade the closer she got.

And on her completely bald head she had the same patterns of white marks as her husband. The patterns shifted as she moved her head slowly from one side to the other, making different scenes.

Searchlights were a race that no one in the superheroes and gods seemed to know much about, or even where on Earth they lived. They seemed to exist in nowhere land.

The Searchlights were called the guardians of the human race, and usually worked with the different deities when a problem threatened humanity.

I first met her husband, Wolfgang Sucker, during the big fight against the Fuzzy-Wuzzy bugs from another dimension. He had been assigned to the Gambling Gods, and since as Poker Boy, I work for them, I got a chance to work with him.

"Poker Boy," the female Searchlight said, her voice as raspy as her husband's, and her breath just as bad. "My name is Emmanuel Sucker, the wife, as you humans would call it, of Wolfgang Sucker."

I wanted to back away to get out of the smell of rotted garlic and dead fish that was her breath, but instead I somehow managed to bow slightly as is a traditional show of respect when talking to a Searchlight.

Then I said, "Very nice to meet you."

"My husband spoke highly of you and your team in our last mating."

I opened my mouth to say something, then closed it and decided that a nod was safer. I was learning far more about the Searchlight society and relationships than I wanted to at that moment. And any question I might ask might cause a lot of problems – or more likely, answers I just didn't want to hear.

And I didn't need my imagination going any farther thinking about a tall pink woman and blue man mating, constantly turning their heads from side to side.

"I need to talk to Front Desk Girl, if you don't mind?" Emmanuel Sucker asked.

"Of course," I said. "Would you wait here while I jump and get her? It will take only a moment."

She nodded.

I knew exactly where Patty was, and could have easily marched the ten or fifteen steps to the front desk and asked for her, but I wanted to practice my newly discovered superpower of jumping around in space.

And besides, when a Searchlight started asking to talk with other superheroes, it usually meant they wanted to talk to the major gods as well. And that meant something very bad was about to happen to humanity in general.

So I winked out, appearing beside Patty in the employee lounge at the same moment taking us out of time so that no other employee saw me appear.

Taking myself out of time used to be my most fun superpower before I learned how to jump around in space. Now I was doing both and that just made me happy. It's not often a simple poker player can learn to teleport and step between moments in time.

Around us a half-dozen of Patty's co-employees were frozen in positions of that moment in time. One woman was chewing on a candy bar and her mouth was half open and it wasn't a pretty sight.

"I love doing that," I said, smiling at the Patty's wonderful brown eyes. She had her long brown hair let down and was wearing the standard black slacks and white blouse of the MGM front desk employee.

"You are getting pretty good at it," Patty said, smiling and kissing me. "Just like many other things."

I think I blushed. In fact I was sure I blushed. And that

simple hint of suggestion almost made me forget about Emmanuel Sucker standing in the front lobby.

"We have a problem," I said. "Did you know Searchlights have mates?"

"No, I didn't," Patty said, frowning. Even with a frown on her face, she was the best-looking woman I had ever seen.

"Well, they do, and Emmanuel Sucker, Wolfgang Sucker's wife, is out front in the lobby and wants to talk to you."

Patty's eyes got wide. "Me? Why?"

"I didn't ask."

Patty was a superhero like I was. There was little if any reason a Searchlight would ask for one of us.

Then I looked up and shouted "Stan! Need help!"

Patty nodded and I flicked us back to a position in front of the Searchlight, then took all three of us out of time so we could talk without all the noise of the lobby.

An instant later, Stan, the God of Poker, joined us, going through the ritual slight bowing to the Searchlight.

Then Emmanuel Sucker, her bald purple head moving slowly from side to side, the patterns on her head moving and changing, bowed slightly to Patty. "Thank you for seeing me."

Patty bowed slightly in return. "It is my honor to meet you. What can we do for you? Is there a problem we are going to need help with?"

"To be most honest," Emmanuel said to Patty, the patterns on her head seeming to move slightly faster than normal, "I only need your help concerning a problem with my husband."

I glanced at Stan, who looked as shocked as I felt.

As far as the little bit of history I knew, no Searchlight had ever come to just talk with one superhero before. They always contacted superheroes first to be taken to the higher gods of each deity. Sort of like going to a servant to be taken to the Queen.

"That will be no problem," Patty said. She turned to Stan. "Can you jump Mrs. Sucker and myself to the meeting room off the main corridor near the lobby? I will call for you when we are finished."

Stan nodded, and an instant later the two women were gone.

"You have any idea what that is about?" Stan asked.

"No more than you do," I said.

He nodded, then said, "I had better tell Laverne and Patty's boss what's happening."

Then he too was gone.

Chapter 2

I let myself drop back into real time.

The sounds of the lobby of the MGM Grand smashed into me. It was always a shock going from the complete silence of between-time and back to real time when it came to the noise. All the people who had been frozen in mid-stride or mid-sentence a moment before were now suddenly moving and talking again.

I stood against the stone pillar off to one side of the grand lobby, no longer waiting for Patty to get off work, but to work her superhero magic with a Searchlight.

I had a sinking feeling about this, and I couldn't tell if that sinking feeling was one of my superpowers trying to warn me, or my normal guy worries about his girlfriend being in some sort of trouble.

I was just starting to try to sort that out when Stan

appeared again and took us back out of time, freezing all the movement in the lobby and silencing all the noise.

"I talked to Laverne," he said. "She didn't seem worried, and told me to keep her informed."

Laverne was Lady Luck herself, one of the most powerful gods anywhere.

"Did you tell Judy what was happening?" I asked.

Judy was the God of Hospitality, the top deity that covered everything to do with lodging and guests staying anywhere. Patty was a superhero under the hospitality gods, working directly under the God of Front Desks, Benson, just like I worked directly under Stan, the God of Poker.

"All Judy said was she was wondering when this was going to happen," Stan said, "and told me to keep her informed as well."

"What was going to happen?" I asked.

Stan shrugged. "Now you know exactly as much as I do. Neither of them would say another word."

"Did you know Searchlights were married?" I asked Stan.

"I assumed they had something like that, otherwise how would they have little Searchlights."

"I thought they lived forever."

"No one lives forever," Stan said. "Even Gods have to be born."

I just shook my head as Stan dropped us back into real time and everyone in the lobby started moving again and the noise of regular people doing regular things washed over us.

We both leaned back against the stone pillar and using the

skill of calm that all good poker players have, we just waited while Patty talked with the bright pink Mrs. Sucker.

But I had to say, the curiosity was killing me.

And the worry for Patty was making my stomach twist into knots.

Chapter 3

About fifteen minutes of intense worry later, Stan nodded to something I couldn't hear and jumped us both to the meeting room.

Patty was alone, sitting at the head of the long oak table in the ornate MGM Grand meeting room. The only sign that Emmanuel Sucker had been there was the lingering odor of her bad breath.

Patty looked worried and tired. I had rarely seen her look like that.

"She wants a place to live," Patty said, looking up at me and giving me a tired smile. "And a job."

Okay, I had to admit, my mouth sort of gaped open at that. The idea of a Searchlight wanting a job was just nuts. They were the beings that Gods bowed to, that watched over humanity against all the threats that might harm us regular people.

Why would Emmanuel Sucker, a Searchlight, need a place to live and a job?

Patty signed and said, "She wants to live here in Vegas for the next twenty-one plus years. She likes it here. And she's pregnant."

Like that was going to explain everything.

"You mean Wolfgang kicked her out for getting pregnant?" I asked.

Behind me Laverne and Judy both laughed.

Stan and I both spun around, moving quickly aside to let Lady Luck and the God of Hospitality closer to Patty. There was a real disadvantage to jumping through space. You could really sneak up on someone. And those two had snuck up on both me and the God of Poker.

Lady Luck had on a black pants suit and black business jacket and looked like every powerful businesswoman tended to look. And she was thin enough and had her hair pulled back tight, making her look like she was even more in control of everything.

Judy, on the other hand, looked like everyone's image of a matronly grandmother. She was even wearing an apron over her plaid dress. And Judy was way, way overweight, something you didn't see often in the Gods.

"How far along is she?" Laverne asked Patty as she and Judy sat down on either side of Patty.

"Two months," Patty said. "She and Wolfgang were

picked for the honor right after the battle with the Fuzzy-Wuzzy."

"So we're going to have to move rather quickly," Judy said, nodding and smiling like this was the best news she had ever heard. "She's going to be leaving home within the next month at most."

Patty nodded. "She says she's already beginning to change. She feels she has less than a week."

Both Laverne and Judy nodded sagely, clearly thinking. About what, I had no clue at all.

I glanced at Stan and he was looking just as puzzled as I felt. But darned if I was going to ask any more stupid questions after my last one.

"First things first," Judy said. "We need to get her a house that she can use for a home for the next twenty-one plus years at a rental payment. The Searchlights will not take any charity from any human or god, even though they help us all the time."

Laverne nodded and turned and looked at me. "Poker Boy, would you mind being Emmanuel's landlord? You and Patty could find her a comfortable home and get her approval before buying it. And make sure it's in a good school district."

Now it was Patty's turn to look puzzled at me.

I had just kept forgetting to tell her that even though I lived in an old double-wide trailer next to a casino in the Oregon coast mountain range, I was very, very rich. She had always just assumed I was a poor poker player. Actually, my poker playing had made me very, very rich; I just seldom spent any of my money.

I had always meant to tell her, but the subject just never came up.

"I'd be honored to do so," I said to Lady Luck.

Laverne nodded. "Make sure her rent is reasonable, but not too low."

Then Laverne turned to Judy, the God of Hospitality. "You think Emmanuel could find a job in your area?"

"I'm sure she could," Judy said. "But with those looks and that build, she might be better served dealing cards. Tips would be a lot better and she would be more comfortable then with the monetary aspects of living here."

I wanted to know how a bright pink bald woman who always turned her head slowly from side-to-side and had horrid breath could deal cards, but I kept my mouth shut again.

"Actually, Judy" Laverne said, nodding, "you are right." Lady Luck turned to Stan. "After Emmanuel is settled, I'll leave it up to you to teach her how to deal poker so she is ready to go after the baby is old enough for her to go to work. I'll loan her some money to last her until then."

"A couple of quick questions," Stan said.

I wanted to say, "Thank you." I had a hundred questions, but I just didn't have the guts to ask anything. Even Patty was looking relieved that she wasn't the one to ask some of the more obvious questions.

Laverne and Judy both laughed at even that much from

Stan. For some reason all this was just too much fun for the two of them, while it was driving the rest of us crazy.

"Shall we tell them?" Laverne asked, clearly enjoying the frowns on our faces.

Judy nodded. "I sure don't see why not. Might help them sleep tonight."

Laverne laughed and then said, "When a Searchlight becomes pregnant, she basically turns into a human. Emmanuel will lose her color and grow hair on her head in the next few weeks."

Well, that was going to help with the poker dealing.

The God of Hospitality smiled and said, "Emmanuel will give birth to a normal-looking human child and will need to raise her child with humans until the child's twenty-first birthday. Then they will both regain their color and head patterns and join their own kind."

"Why?" Patty asked a half second before Stan and I could.

"This has always been their way," Laverne said, "from the beginning of humanity. It allows them to understand those they are protecting."

"When was the last Searchlight born?" Patty asked.

"There hasn't been a new Searchlight baby since the days of Atlantis," Judy said. "But I expect more in the next few centuries; maybe one even sooner, since this child will need a mate."

"And Poker Boy," Laverne said, smiling at me, "you might consider including Emmanuel on your team in the future for some missions. She will have some special powers, although it might take a little time to figure out exactly what they are."

"Be glad to," I said, trying to imagine Emmanuel Sucker joining the rest of us at The Diner for milkshakes while we tried to solve dangerous problems.

"Keep us informed as to your progress," Laverne said.

Patty and I and Stan all nodded and an instant later the two major gods were gone.

"Too weird, just too weird," Stan said, shaking his head and then he also vanished, leaving me with my wonderful girlfriend.

I dropped into the chair beside Patty. "You all right?"

She nodded. "Just stunned is all. Not sure why Emmanuel picked me."

"I think her husband liked you," I said, smiling.

"Looks like we will have a new charge very shortly," Patty said. "And maybe a new member of the team."

"Could be interesting," I said, still not sure how she might help us. But she was a Searchlight. Even a human Searchlight might be of help.

"I have a hunch," Patty said, "from a few things Emmanuel mentioned, that she will need lots of coaching in our modern world."

"Breath mints as well," I said.

"We can hope that changes with her skin color," Patty said.

Patty then turned to face me, a serious look on her face.

"Laverne wants you to buy Emmanuel Sucker a house? You want to explain how that is possible?"

I sort of coughed under the intense gaze of those superhero brown eyes. "I can easily afford it," I said, smiling. "You know, poker winnings."

"I think we need to talk," Patty said, clearly not happy that I hadn't told her I had money.

Lots and lots of money. So much money, in fact, I wasn't sure how much I had anymore.

But I had a hunch, since Patty was a hundred years older than I was, that there were some things she hasn't told me as well. It might be a very, very interesting conversation, one we had needed to have for a while now.

"Your place or my trailer?" I asked, smiling.

She just glared at me, clearly not even happy at the question. So I picked her place and jumped us there.

Just safer.

And somewhere I was sure I could hear Lady Luck and the God of Hospitality laughing.

NOT SALEABLE
FOR SALE

CHAPTER ONE

Seeing a leprechaun appear in a small casino in the mountains of Oregon can make even a professional poker player like me lose my train of thought.

I flipped my A-10 off-suit into the muck and turned to my right as the leprechaun waved at me.

He had on the standard, leprechaun-green top hat that didn't cover his pointed ears but sort of rode on them like they were training wheels for the big hat. He had a green jacket, brown pants, and a long-stemmed pipe in his mouth that didn't seem to be lit. It stuck out of his scraggly red beard like a weed out of a ragged lawn.

He wasn't any taller than the back of a poker chair, and was as skinny as a flagpole. Somehow he climbed onto a chair, on top of an empty poker table, and then sat down, his big brown shoes with gold buckles dangling over the edge of the table like he was a kid sitting in a huge chair.

I glanced around to see if anyone else had noticed the new visitor.

No one had, even though there were three tables of eight going at the moment. Spirit Winds Casino in the Oregon mountains didn't have many people in the poker room at midnight on a Wednesday.

I was here because I was just waiting for my girlfriend to get off work at the MGM Grand Casino in Las Vegas, and I figured the plucking of tourists would be easier here tonight than in Vegas. And since, as Poker Boy, I could jump back and forth instantly with my Jump Anywhere Power, it didn't matter where I played.

Besides, this was my old home casino; I knew everyone here, and it was comfortable. There was a lot to be said about comfort.

Now a stupid leprechaun had interrupted my nice evening.

I had only seen leprechauns in Vegas at the Okey-Doke Casino out on the old highway. It was one of those places hidden with magic, so that no one knew it was there unless you were taken there. I had helped solve a big problem there a while back, so maybe this guy was just coming to say hi and thank me again.

I doubted it. I had learned that no one could ever trust a leprechaun. And I had no plan on trusting this one, either.

I pushed away from the table and tossed the dealer a ten-dollar chip. "If I'm not back in thirty minutes, rack them and hold them for me, would you?"

The dealer nodded and rapped the chip on the felt in acknowledgement.

I adjusted my black leather coat and zipped it up, then made sure my black fedora-like hat was on solid before turning away from the table.

Already the little skinny guy had cost me money. My hunch was it was only going to go downhill from here.

"Where'd you leave the pot of gold?" I asked as I walked past him.

"Funny," he said, his voice deep and raspy and not fitting his thin, small body at all. "Very damn funny."

Leprechauns hated being teased about their pots of gold. They had lost all of it, every damn pot, a couple of centuries before in a bad bet with a few aliens who happened to be visiting Earth at the time. It was still a touchy subject.

I just kept walking, letting him jump down from the table and follow me. I had no intention of carrying on a conversation with an invisible man while on casino security cameras. That wouldn't do my reputation any good at all.

Besides, I needed a break and some fresh air.

At a fast walk, I weaved my way through the slot machines, cutting through all the smoke and older people plugging the machines like the world was about to end and they wanted to get rid of every dollar before it did.

As we neared the front door of the casino, the little guy finally caught up with me, his pipe in one hand, his other hand holding his hat onto his head as he ran. He was panting and swearing lightly under his breath.

"Shouldn't smoke so much," I said as I pushed open the door and hesitated to let him go through ahead of me.

"You shouldn't be such a jerk," the little guy said in his deep voice. He sounded more like a country-western singer and he didn't have any accent at all.

"You're the one who is bothering me," I said, heading out toward the parking lot to where I knew there was a small dead spot in the security cameras. The fall night air felt great after wading through the smoke around those slot machines. Clean and pure.

I glanced at my watch. Still over two hours before I had to pick up Patty at the MGM Grand.

Patty was also called Front Desk Girl, and she was a super-hero in the hospitality part of the gambling universe. We fit together perfectly and made a great team. She had long brown hair and wonderful brown eyes I loved getting lost in. She was only a few inches shorter than I was, but when she wore heels we seemed to be the same size.

"I just came to ask for help from the *great* Poker Boy," the leprechaun said.

"Sarcasm just won't get me doing anything," I said. "So what's your name?"

He glared at me. I knew that knowing any magical creature's name gave me power over them. And he knew I knew it. He had no intention of giving me that kind of power.

"So what do I call you?" I asked.

"Lenny," he said. He clearly must have already figured that's the name he would use with me.

"Lenny the Leprechaun," I said, shaking my head as I reached the dead area in the security cameras and stopped, sitting down on the edge of a planter to be more at his level. "Got it."

"I'm an elf," he said, getting red in the face and spreading his thin legs into a fighting stance in front of me. Old elves who wore green and smoked pipes for some reason never liked to be called leprechauns. No one had explained that to me yet. Someday I would ask Stan, the God of Poker why that was.

"Sorry," I said. "So what can I do for you?"

Lenny took the pipe out of his mouth and stuck it in his belt, then adjusted his tall hat and then his green vest. Then he went to pacing in front of me, two steps, turn, two steps. With his short legs he didn't go far in either direction.

He clearly didn't want to tell me why he had come to find me.

I clicked on my Trust Me super power," added a little Calming Power and aimed it at him.

He suddenly stopped pacing and faced me.

"Nice magic," he said, taking a deep breath and clearly relaxing. "Thanks, I feel better."

I had never thought of my powers as magic before, but I

suppose they were. And I had never tried them on a magical creature before now. Learn something every day, even from a Leprechaun.

"You're welcome," I said, switching off my power. "Now, what's happening?"

"Mrs. Lenny, my wife, is missing."

CHAPTER TWO

Now, of all the things a leprechaun might come to me for help with, I sure would have never thought it would be to find his wife. I didn't even know where leprechauns lived. I had heard that the ones around Vegas lived in magically hidden forests and glens in valleys up by Lake Mead. But I would have to ask someone above me in the ranks if even that was right.

And besides, I was a superhero in the world of gambling, specializing in poker, thus the name, Poker Boy. I wasn't Missing-Persons-Boy, although I wouldn't be surprised that a superhero with that name actually existed. Gods and superheroes seemed to exist for just about everything on the planet.

So he had to have a special reason for coming to me.

"I'm sorry to hear about your wife," I said, actually being sincere. "But not sure what you think I can do to help."

"I was told you would be the best person to help me," he said, looking very worried.

"Who told you that?" More than likely this was just a joke being played on me, and so far I had fallen for it and taken the little guy a little too seriously.

"The general manager of the Okey-Doke Casino checked around and found out you were the best. He asked your boss if it would be all right if I contacted you, and he said sure."

"My boss?" I asked, now stunned. "Who do you think my boss is?"

The little guy sort of shrugged. "Some guy named Stan I think."

That was enough. I looked up into the air and shouted "Stan!"

An instant later Stan, the God of Poker, appeared beside me in the parking lot. He had on his normal brown slacks, short-sleeved business shirt that matched his slacks and loafers. He had nothing at all distinctive about his face and his brown hair was cut short, but not too short. Perfect camouflage for a poker player. He could walk down the street and no one would notice him.

Stan glanced around and nodded. "Dead camera area, huh?"

"And fresh air," I said.

"A little chilly," he said and a brown sweater appeared on him.

"You know Lenny here," I said, indicating the leprechaun.

Stan nodded. "Never met, but heard of the problem.

Sorry to hear about your wife. If anyone can help you, it's Poker Boy."

Okay, so now I was convinced that Stan was in on this joke as well. Gods were well known for pulling pranks and practical jokes. And Stan had done his share over the years.

I stood, adjusting my leather coat. "Okay, so tell me the punch line so I can get back to my game."

Lenny the Leprechaun looked pained and Stan just looked puzzled. After a moment Stan seemed to catch on to what I was saying, and he shook his head and looked at Lenny.

"You haven't told him your problem yet?"

"I told him my wife was missing," he said, defensively.

"But you didn't tell him where, did you?" Stan asked, staring down at the little elf.

Lenny looked almost insulted. "Where else would my wife go missing that I couldn't find her?"

I shook my head and started away from the dead area of the casino parking lot. "I've got a game to finish."

"Silicon Suckers," Stan said.

The two words stopped me cold and I turned around and went back.

Silicon Suckers are a very, very old race of beings that have been on Earth far longer than humans. They are often mistaken for the "Grays" by alien-watchers. The Silicon Suckers live in what they call "castles" under desert areas. They have huge, city-sized caverns and hundreds of miles of tunnels under the desert outside of Vegas on the north side of town. The Silicon Suckers control a large amount of desert all around Las Vegas. I have done numbers of favors for them over the years, so I am an honored guest in their cities.

They also killed an old girlfriend of mine when she wouldn't return some sacred silicon a doctor had put into her breasts. I had warned her many times that the Silicon Suckers would get their silicon back one way or another. And they did.

I ignored Lenny and looked at Stan. "I thought the fairy world and the Silicon Suckers were not on speaking terms."

"They aren't," Stan said, clearly disgusted. "But Mrs. Lenny thought she might be able to negotiate with them for a small piece of property near the lake."

"Did she ask *anyone* why that property would never be for sale?" I asked, stunned. The only property the Silicon Suckers controlled near Lake Mead was a cliff face that represented some of their deepest beliefs and history. I was told that the cliff was the last remaining wall of their most ancient city.

"I doubt it," Stan said. "Otherwise she wouldn't be missing."

"We thought it would be a good addition to a charming pool under the wall," Lenny said. "Make some slides on it, diving platforms, you know the drill."

I just shook my head in disgust. Stan just smiled. His poker face was better than mine.

If Lenny's wife had tried to even make an offer on that cliff face, she was long since dead. Just the offer would be so insulting to the Silicon Suckers that Lenny's wife would be moisture for their underground gardens.

I was about to tell Lenny that, when it dawned on me that I knew exactly where Lenny's wife was, and that she hadn't even gotten to insulting the Silicon Suckers by telling them her people wanted to make a recreational area out of a scared place.

I started laughing and both Stan and Lenny looked at me like I had gone crazy.

"Where did she try to go in?" I asked Lenny between laughs.

"At the large *Downtown Vegas* billboard off the highway on the north," Lenny said, staring at me. "And what's so damned funny about my wife being missing?"

"She's not dead, that's what," I said. "She is a magical being, right?"

"Of course," Lenny said, clearly angry, his little frame shaking.

Then Stan started laughing as well. He understood enough about the Silicon Suckers to know that they must know a person's true name before they will be allowed inside of their castles. And magical people won't give out their real names unless really pressed, thus she would never be allowed into any Silicon Sucker city.

"I'll go get her," I said to Stan. "Take Lenny here back to Vegas and wait for my shout."

Chapter Three

Stan nodded and I jumped to a small café on a side street in downtown Vegas. "The Diner" was my team's favorite hangout, and it had the best hamburgers and milkshakes in town. It was decorated like one of the old 1960s diners, and was run by Madge, a superhero in the food service world.

When I appeared, Madge was behind the counter and there were no other customers in the place. Madge had her hair up like normal in a tight bun, and her brown waitress dress was two sizes too small as was always normal as well.

She turned around and smiled. "I was expecting you, Poker Boy," she said. "I heard that little leprechaun fellow was going to ask you to help rescue his wife from the Silicon Suckers."

"Word travels fast," I said, smiling as she placed three thermoses of hot chocolate on the counter in front of me.

She knew that hot chocolate was the drug of choice for Silicon Suckers. It was more precious to them then gold was to humans. I had watched one Silicon Sucker take just a drop of hot chocolate and go into orgasmic shudders.

Three thermoses full would give me some real bargaining power for Mrs. Lenny.

"Thanks, Madge," I said, dropping a hundred dollar bill on the counter. "Does that cover everything?"

She smiled and picked up the bill. "More than enough."

Now I was down a hundred and ten for this adventure.

"See you soon," I said.

I put one thermos into each pocket of my leather coat and then held the other one and jumped to the billboard on the highway.

The lights of the billboard lit up the surrounding highway, and a moment after I arrived on the sand under the billboard a car sped past, headed out of town. The driver must have gotten a shock me appearing in front of him like that.

The air was cold and the wind light, but brisk. I was glad I had on my coat. The high-desert winter cold wasn't far away.

I moved over to where I knew the entrance of the Silicon Sucker's city was, in the side of a sand hillside about twenty feet from the billboard.

A huge pair of high-heeled shoes lay there in the sand. And when I say huge, I don't mean size twelve. Those things would be considered small boats for some people and I had no doubt that Lenny could put both feet into one shoe and have room to move his toes around. If leprechauns even had toes.

I didn't see any tiny leprechaun shoes nearby, so I moved to the entrance, kicked off my own tennis shoes, and then bowed at the empty night air.

"Poker Boy would request the honor of entering a sacred city of the honorable Silicon Suckers. I have brought a gift."

I bowed slightly and held up the thermos of hot chocolate.

A second later the opening to the Silicon Sucker underground city appeared and I stepped inside.

I was met ten steps inside by two Silicon Suckers. They bowed and wished me long life and a pleasant visit to their city.

I handed over my thermos of hot chocolate and the two carried it away carefully, both holding it like it was a bomb and might explode.

A moment later another Silicon Sucker appeared and bowed to me slightly. "It is a pleasure to see you again, Poker Boy."

"The pleasure is mine," I said, bowing as well. All Silicon Suckers looked pretty much the same, so I had no idea if I had met this one before or not.

He turned and I followed him through the narrow tunnel to a larger tunnel where a very, very large woman knelt on the sand floor looking very, very tired. At least she had not yet committed the deadly sin of falling asleep or leaning against a wall. She knew that much it seemed about Silicon Sucker rules.

Even kneeling and slumping, she was taller than I was, and I could barely fit in these tunnels. She must have walked on her knees just to get this far.

She was wearing a brown dress that looked dusty, and her hair was curly brown and short against her head. She had a very wide face with a nose that seemed to spread from one cheek to the other. At one point she had had on make-up, but that had run with tears.

I was almost afraid to ask, but I did anyway. "Is your husband a leprechaun?"

She looked over at me, startled, clearly seeing me for the first time. Then she smiled. "He is."

I turned to my host and spoke in Silicon Sucker native. "I have come to bargain for this being's release from your wonderful city. Her husband has need of her at home."

"She will not tell us her name," my host said.

I had no doubt they had not even asked, but had just expected it.

"It is against her culture," I said.

"Then we cannot release her."

I knew better at that moment to insult him by trying to bribe him with the hot chocolate in my coat.

"If she tells you her real name, will she be allowed to leave your fine city?"

"We will consider it," my host said.

I turned to Mrs. Lenny who was looking at me with

horror since I had spoken to the Silicon Sucker in his own language of strange ticks and snorts and hisses.

"If you tell this one Silicon Sucker your real name, you may be able to leave."

She started to object, but I held up my hand for her to stop.

"I will cover my ears to make sure I have not heard your name. I know doing so is against your beliefs, but if you want to live, you now have no choice. I will never mention to anyone you have done so."

She again started to speak but again I stopped her with a raised hand.

"If you complain, I may not be able to get you out of here at all. Say nothing to this Silicon Sucker but *My name is... I am honored in your presence.*"

She nodded.

"And do not lie. It must be your full name. They will know if it is not. Nod only if you understand."

She nodded again.

"I will cover my ears now, you will state your full and real name. Then I will bargain for your release."

I could tell she was so tired, she didn't care anymore. I knew she was violating something that was important, but at this point she just had no choice if she wanted to see little Lenny again.

I covered my ears and after a moment I could see her speaking.

When she stopped the Silicon Sucker bowed to her and I

knew her name had been a true one.

I turned to my host. "I have a gift for my host in exchange for the release of this being."

I removed another thermos of hot chocolate.

"Is her life worth such a price?" he asked.

"It is," I said. "And for allowing me to speak on her behalf, I have another gift for my wonderful friends."

I pulled out the other thermos of hot chocolate.

I thought my host might actually gasp. But somehow he maintained his poise and nodded. "Your friend may leave with you, Poker Boy."

"Thank you," I said, bowing.

"And you are always a welcomed, honored guest in our castles."

At that moment two other Silicon Suckers appeared and took the two thermoses from me, then the three of them walked away.

I held up my hand that Mrs. Lenny should not speak, then indicated that she should follow me back toward the entrance.

She did, somehow walking on her knees without touching either the walls or the floor with her hands. I had no doubt those sand burns on her knees were going to take some time to heal.

When we got outside, the entrance behind us vanished and she fell panting into the sand.

"Stan!" I said into the air.

Stan and Lenny the Leprechaun appeared. Lenny rushed

to the huge woman and tried to hug her. He managed to sort of hug one arm.

Then he tried to help her to her feet and somehow managed to not get crushed.

Standing up in bare feet, Mrs. Lenny the Leprechaun stood a good twelve feet tall. She could change the light bulbs on the billboard without a ladder if she wanted to.

She rested her hand gently on her husband's shoulder while he sort of hugged her thigh.

"Thank you," she said in a very high, faint voice.

"Yes, thank you," Lenny said in a very low voice, nodding to me. "They were right about you, Poker Boy."

"Let's go home," Mrs. Lenny said, indicating that Lenny should pick up her shoes.

"Anything you say, my little sweetness," Lenny said and he managed to heft both shoes and they vanished.

I looked at Stan, shocked.

And he looked back at me, clearly just as shocked.

"You didn't tell me Mrs. Lenny Leprechaun was a giant," I said.

"I didn't know," Stan said, shaking his head.

Then, before we both broke down laughing right there outside of the Silicon Suckers castle, I picked up my shoes and said, "Meet you after two at The Diner?"

He nodded about to break down in laughter and I jumped back to the parking lot of my favorite casino in Oregon.

I laughed all the way inside trying to keep my imagination from running wild and failing miserably.

I collected my chips that had been racked for me. I was just over a hundred up for the night, so I ended up only slightly behind for the evening with all the rescue expenses.

When I jumped to pick up Patty at the MGM Grand in Vegas, I gave her a hug. She fit perfectly in my arms and I started laughing again thinking of Lenny hugging his wife's thigh.

"What's so funny?" Patty asked looking up at me with those wonderful brown eyes of hers.

"I just like the way we fit together is all," I said.

"So do I," she said, giving me a hug. "Are you propositioning a very tired woman?"

Suddenly the image of Lenny and his wife in bed together went through my mind and I shuddered.

A really bad reaction to what Patty had asked.

Really bad.

And it took me and Stan both to the end of hamburgers and milkshakes at The Diner to explain.

The Smoke That Doesn't Bark

Chapter One

As a superhero in the gambling universe, I have no idea why I always end up saving dogs. It sure seems that every time there is a person for me to save there is also a dog that needs my help. Not always, but my sidekick, Patty Ledgerwood, aka Front Desk Girl, thought it funny because it happens so often. And as she said, "It's kinda sweet."

Sometimes the person who needs the help owns the dog, other times the dog is not related in any way to the person I'm trying to help. I asked my boss, Stan, the God of Poker, about it once and he just thought I was kidding. It seems that animals have their own gods that take care of them.

Stan told me that over the years there has been very little reason for the Gambling Gods to associate with the Gods of

Animals and Reptiles. That made sense to me considering animals are not known for placing bets.

But sometimes the lines between the different branches of gods are not as clear as some people make them out to be.

It was New Year's Eve, or more accurately, two in the morning on New Year's Day. One of my favorite things to do on New Year's Eve was to play a tournament at the MGM Grand on the strip in Vegas. Granted, that is a long way from my double-wide mobile home near a large Indian casino in Oregon, but Patty lives and works in Vegas, so I look for any reason to visit her as often as I can.

I must confess that Patty and I have a relationship. Sometimes that isn't smart between superhero and sidekick. But she's actually a superhero as well, working under the God of Hospitality. And we aren't serious enough yet for me to move from Oregon to Vegas. We have talked about it, sure, just not there yet.

By Vegas standards, the New Year's Eve tournament wasn't a big event, not like others around town, but for the past ten years I had made the little tournament at the MGM Grand on New Year's Eve a tradition, and I like tradition. And since half the people playing in the tournament were drunk tourists, and most of the professional poker players were at the bigger tournaments at other casinos, it made getting into the money fairly easy. In fact, I had made the final table and the money every year.

Besides, I love the sounds of a casino alive with people laughing and talking and machine bells going off, and on

New Year's Eve, all that seemed to be more in focus, sharper, and if possible, louder.

The money was always nice as well, since the MGM Grand also kicked in a few grand added money. I have nothing against making some money in a decent poker game. After all, superheroes have to make a living to pay for chasing after the bad guys. Most people thought the gods paid for the superheroes working for them, but they sure don't. We are expected to make a living and solve everyone's problems at the same time.

Considering that I make my living playing poker, I'm not complaining.

But Patty had to work tonight on her new job at the front desk of the MGM Grand, and she wouldn't be off until 3 a.m., at which time we would head to her wonderful apartment and enjoy the first day of the New Year together.

So I still had an hour, and had made the final table of the tournament. In fact, I was chip leader, and planned on using my chip advantage over the other eight players at the table to eventually take all their chips. In less than an hour, I hoped.

Suddenly, the dealer froze in the middle of her deal, the card suspended in midair, her nose scrunched up in concentration. All the loud noise of the casino and the laughing and talking cut off like I had been transported to an empty desert without any wind.

Around the table the players' faces were frozen in the moment. I had learned over the years that when you freeze a person in a moment, they seldom look good. A person's looks are dependent on movement. If you don't believe me, just randomly stop your DVD player with an attractive person on screen. Chances are their eyes will be rolled into their head slightly, their mouths open in a doofy fashion, and their expression twisted. The eight other players at the table and the dealer were no exceptions to the "frozen uglies" as I liked to call what they looked like.

Someone had taken me out of time and I only knew of a few people beside me that had that power, so I glanced around. Stan, the God of Poker, was winding his way through the frozen-in-time players, clearly headed my way. Another silver-haired man was walking a few steps behind him.

The guy had large and slanted dark eyes, set far enough apart that, for a second, I wondered if he could see in two directions at once. He was dressed in a dark silk suit and matching tie that shouted money and power. He moved so smoothly behind Stan I wasn't sure he was even walking.

"Poker Boy," Stan said as I stood and stepped toward them, "meet The Smoke."

The Smoke just nodded and didn't bother to step close enough to shake my hand, so I didn't offer. I had a very odd feeling about the guy, but couldn't place it, which made me even more uncomfortable. As a poker player, my greatest strength was easily summing up a person and figuring them out. This guy would be tough across a poker table.

Now understand I didn't dislike the guy. I just couldn't get a read on him.

"I'm assuming there's a problem," I said to Stan, adjusting

my superhero costume, which consisted of a black leather coat and black Fedora-like hat. My six-foot height made me about five inches taller than the compact frame of The Smoke. For some reason that pleased me.

"Let's walk," Stan said. "We need to meet Patty."

If Stan was putting both of us on a case, something really important had gone wrong.

Really important.

I pointed at my stack of tournament chips on the table. "Release the room and I'll tell them to blind me off. I'll follow you in a moment."

Blinding off a stack meant that a player in a tournament still had to pay the blinds every round, even if they weren't in the chair. So my chip stack would dwindle slowly until gone while all my hands would be folded.

Stan nodded and turned to leave. I sat back down just as he released the freeze and let me drop back into normal time. The sounds of the casino came crashing back in like a hammer and every face around the table returned to normal.

I quickly stood again and nodded to the dealer. "Blind me off until I get back."

She nodded and I turned and headed out of the poker room. Unless I got back quickly, I wouldn't win the tournament, but with the size of my stack, just being blinded off slowly might get me third or fourth as other players knocked themselves out. Still a decent payday for my New Year's tradition.

I was about halfway to the lobby of the casino when

everything around me froze again and the noise vanished once more. Stan and Patty and The Smoke were standing in the middle of the wide aisle near the huge, open hotel lobby, talking.

Patty looked better than ever. I had first met her five years back when she worked downtown at the Horseshoe, the last year the World Series of Poker was held there. Tonight the white blouse and dark pants accented her perfectly trim body in a way I very much liked. Her long brown hair was tied back and up, giving her a serious look.

I know it sounds corny, but every time I saw her, my heart sort of raced, and this time was no exception, even though I had talked to her just an hour ago during one of the tournament breaks.

Patty glanced over at me with her large brown eyes and smiled a smile that could melt anyone into a puddle on the ornate tile floor. "You winning?"

"Of course," I said, laughing. "Chip leader. Final table just got started."

"Sorry," Stan said.

I just shrugged. "Work needs to come first. So what's the problem?"

Stan glanced at The Smoke, then said simply, "About two hours ago, someone placed a number of very large bets with a number of bookmakers around town that all the dogs in North America would be killed at exactly twelve noon on the first day of the year, Vegas time."

Patty gasped and I tried to understand what Stan had just said. "All the dogs? Why?"

"No one knows," Stan said.

"That's just sick," Patty said.

The Smoke seemed to be showing no emotion at all. He just stood there, his thin, dark, wide-set eyes seeming to observe everything around him.

The silence of the frozen casino seemed to grow as Patty and I tried to take in what we had been told.

I turned to face The Smoke directly. "I assume you work for the animal gods."

The Smoke nodded. "We are aware of your ability to save dogs," he said, his voice deep and low. "Since this involves a bet, my boss went to Laverne and we asked for your help."

Laverne was Lady Luck herself. I hoped she had a lot more than me and Patty and Stan on this problem.

I nodded and turned to Stan. "I assume you are looking for the guy who placed the bet."

"Oh, we know who it was. He has nothing to do with the coming deaths. He's just trying to make some huge money on it to rebuild his house."

"The Bookkeeper!" both Patty and I said at the same time.

Stan nodded and we all went back to being silent. Three months ago the Bookkeeper, while trying to prove to the world that there was no luck, had mathematically trapped Lady Luck herself. Patty and I and Screamer, the third member of my team, had barely rescued her in time. But in the process, the Bookkeeper's home had been completely destroyed, along with all of his super computers and about three bedrooms and a living room full of very smelly trash.

The Bookkeeper had an uncanny ability to predict future events with just math.

"We'll need to talk to him," I said.

Stan nodded. "I'll bring him to you. Where?"

"Does he still smell?" Patty asked about a half-second before I did.

"He smells like a field of lilacs now," Stan said. "Something one of his bosses did to him."

"A small field I hope," I said.

Stan shook his head. "Not so small."

"Oh, wonderful," Patty said.

"Our normal place in fifteen minutes," I told Stan.

Stan nodded.

Our normal place was a small restaurant, open 24 hours a day, called The Diner. It pretended to be an old 1960s diner, and was tucked into a hole on a side street near the old Horseshoe Casino downtown. When the team of Patty and Screamer and I first formed, that's where we met, and it's become our normal meeting site for any case we were working together.

Besides, it had great milkshakes, and right now I could use one.

Stan released the "out of time bubble" on us and Patty and I headed across the lobby toward the exit to the parking area out back, with her explaining how she managed to get off an hour early on her shift tonight. We were most of the way across the hotel lobby when I realized that The Shadow was following us about five feet back, walking as silently as anyone I had ever met.

"Where's Stan?" I asked, turning to him.

"He said I was to help you," The Shadow said, again his voice low and rough and at the same time very smooth. "He said he had a few other leads to check out and would catch up."

I nodded and said, "Sounds fine. More help the better."

I turned back to Patty, who handed me her cell phone as we walked, with The Shadow following a few feet behind us. When I put it to my ear the phone was already ringing.

"Patty," Screamer said as he answered, clearly seeing his caller id. "What's up?" His voice was chipper and I could hear music and laughter behind him.

"Sorry to bother you tonight," I said, "We've got a pretty nasty one."

"Hey, Poker Boy. Great hearing your voice again. When?"

"Fifteen minutes," I said.

"I'll be there," he said and hung up.

I handed Patty back her phone, then said. "The old gang is back together again. I just hope we can pull off another miracle."

"So do I," The Smoke said softly behind us.

CHAPTER TWO

It took us exactly sixteen minutes to get to The Diner downtown from the MGM Grand on the Strip. Screamer was already there and he was sitting in our normal booth, but I indicated we should move to the big table in the corner. The idea of sitting next to the Bookkeeper in a tight booth was nightmarish at best.

Madge, the slightly overweight waitress with far, far too tight slacks walked up, popped her gum, and said, "Well, looks like the Weird Bunch is back in town. And with a new member as well."

"Great seeing you again, Madge," I said. I didn't blame her for being sort of curt with us. Over the years some strange things had happened in this restaurant around us, and we had left unfinished more meals than we had eaten here.

"Milkshakes around?" Madge asked, her gum popping again.

Screamer, Patty and I nodded. The Smoke simply said, "Water. Hamburger very rare, no onion or pickles or anything green on it. Hold the mustard and any other sauce."

Madge took it all down and glanced at The Smoke. "You fit right in with this group. Anyone else?"

We all shook our heads and after Madge left, I introduced The Smoke to Screamer. They didn't shake hands, just nodded at each other.

"I've heard of you," Screamer said, sitting back in his chair. You've rescued more animals than Poker Boy here, and that's going some."

"And I've heard of your ability to get inside someone's head," The Smoke said, nodding in respect. "It is a pleasure to meet you."

The Smoke was talking about Screamer's superpower. He could transfer what one person was thinking to another or read their minds just by a touch. He got his nickname by making a serial killer scream in horror by digging up his worst fears and making him see and live them to get him to confess. His methods never would stand up in court, but it gets the really bad guys off the streets.

Screamer turned to me. "I assume we're dealing with a problem with animals if The Smoke is joining us."

I nodded and quickly outlined what we already knew. I had just finished when the sounds of the restaurant vanished and Stan and The Bookkeeper appeared.

Across the small restaurant, Madge was frozen bending over to pick something off the floor near the cash register. Luckily for all of us, she was slightly behind the counter so we didn't have to see frozen all that her tight outfit exposed.

Suddenly a wave of purple smell hit us. Intensely purple lilac smell.

The Smoke got up and moved quickly to the other side of the table away from Stan and The Bookkeeper, while the three of us instantly covered our noses. I wasn't sure which was worse: the intense smell of rotting food and trash The Bookkeeper used to smell like, or this intense perfume smell of lilacs, so thick I wasn't sure I would ever taste anything but purple again.

"Hey, Poker Boy, Patty, Screamer," the Bookkeeper said. "I never did get to thank you for saving my ass with Lady Luck."

"No problem," I said, then started to say something else and choked on the smell and couldn't speak.

"We'll make this quick," Stan said. "Screamer, would you touch the Bookkeeper and then connect him with Poker Boy." He glanced at Patty and The Smoke. "You two touch Poker Boy so you all get what he knows exactly."

I'd been inside the Bookkeeper's mind once before and I wasn't looking forward to doing it again. I could tell that neither were Patty and Screamer. I had no idea what The Smoke was feeling.

Stan faced the Bookkeeper. "Focus on everything you

know about the coming death of the dogs, including how you worked it out."

The Bookkeeper nodded and Screamer touched his shoulder and then my arm as Patty and The Smoke both touched my shoulders, one on each side.

Like a movie run in fast forward, I could instantly see the Bookkeeper sitting at a computer, his fingers flying as he worked out some sort of equation that I didn't understand. I tried to focus on what facts he was plugging into the equations, but none of it made any sense to me.

At the same time I could sense Patty's mind and Screamer's. Both of them I was used to, but The Smoke was like a dark place in the connection, his mind not really part of the group for some reason or another.

Screamer broke the connection and I shuddered, glad to be out of the Bookkeeper's head once again.

The Bookkeeper looked at Screamer. "That's just so weird."

"Come on," Stan said, and an instant later he and the Bookkeeper were gone and the noise of the restaurant and the street outside flooded back into the silence.

I took a napkin and blew my nose, trying to clear some of the smell without success. I could taste lilacs, and it felt like my skin was coated in the smell, like someone had dumped an entire bottle of cheap perfume over me.

"Anyone get anything out of that?" I asked, "Besides the need for a shower?"

The Smoke came back around the table and sat down

again as we all tried to piece together the thing we had seen in fast motion from the Bookkeeper's mind.

"He seemed to only be working with probability equations," Screamer said.

Patty nodded.

"So what in the world made him even start on those equations?" I asked. "A person like the Bookkeeper just doesn't come up with 'all dogs dying' out of the blue."

We all sat in silence trying to dig back through the wave of information we had all gotten from the connection with the Bookkeeper's mind. It was like trying to sort through a library of information. The closer you looked, if you looked in the wrong spot, the deeper you got into the wrong details.

Like rewinding a DVD, I ran back over the Bookkeeper working on the problem until the moment he first sat down at a computer with the idea. Then I slowed down what I was seeing, still in reverse, until I finally got to the trigger point.

"Oh, no," The Smoke said softly.

He must have gotten to the same point I had managed to get to in the information in our minds.

"How is that possible?" I asked The Smoke.

"What possible?" Patty and Screamer asked at the same moment.

"Please," Patty said. "I don't want to play around in that guy's mind anymore than I have to."

"Basically," I said, glancing at The Smoke, "At noon today all dogs are going to become human. Sort of."

He nodded. "That's what it looks like."

Before I could ask him the dozen questions I had for him, Marge said, "What's that smell?"

She was waving her hand in front of her face while carrying a tray of milkshakes with the other.

"Sorry," I said. "A little perfume bottle accident."

She half-dropped the milkshakes and tray on our table. "Smells more like a perfume factory disaster," she said, heading for the door at full speed. She opened it and blocked it open, then headed for the back room. "Got to get a cross-breeze in here."

I glanced at the milkshake in front of me, but had no desire to drink it at the moment. Not only would it just taste like purple lilacs, but with what we had discovered by putting all the pieces together, the Bookkeeper was going to win his bet.

"Is it possible for a dog to become human?" Screamer asked. "Isn't that something like being a werewolf?"

"Wolves become human, yes," The Smoke said. "I am a werewolf, actually."

I was so startled, I just opened my mouth and then closed it again with no words coming out.

Patty just stared at him.

"Full moon stuff and all?" Screamer asked.

The Smoke, smiled, sort of, without showing his teeth. "No, I can turn at will and have complete control over both forms."

"So is that what's going to happen to all the dogs?" Patty asked. "Are they suddenly going to have your power?"

The Smoke shook his head sadly. "I was a human first before my power came about. Dogs have much smaller brains and would not understand their new form or how to live as humans. They would still have the minds and actions of dogs."

"This is a disaster," Screamer said. "Millions of new humans are suddenly going to appear. Humans that need help and can't take care of themselves as humans. This is going to crash our entire economy."

"So what's causing this?" Patty asked. "Or who? And why?"

"Back to what triggered the Bookkeeper to figure it out," Screamer said.

"No one is causing this. We have no villains," I said and The Smoke nodded.

"Radiation spike," I said. I could see clearly how the Bookkeeper had read a study on a coming short, intense burst of radiation from a cloud in space that the Earth would pass through. The focus of the hit would be the North American continent and it would only last for a fraction of a second exactly at noon Vegas time. Scientists believed it would be harmless and were just planning on studying the coming burst. But when the Bookkeeper learned of the exact frequency of the burst, he started to work the probability equations.

The Smoke just nodded. "The Bookkeeper somehow knew a secret very closely guarded among the animal gods on how to turn an animal human."

"Are more than just dogs going to be changed?" Screamer said. "I'm having a hard time imaging mouse-sized humans running around."

"Luckily, no," The Smoke said. "If the Bookkeeper is correct on the information he has on the frequency and duration of the burst, it will be only dogs. All dogs."

"So what are we going to do?" Patty asked.

I knew exactly what needed to be done. I didn't think it was possible, but I sure hoped it would be.

"We're going to call in the big guns," I said, smiling, remembering what had happened outside of the Bookkeeper's home when it blew up.

"Big Guns?" Screamer asked, looking at me with puzzlement.

I turned to The Smoke. "What level are you over in your world of deities?"

"I'm a superhero like you three," he said. "I can change my shape at will into a dozen different animals, pass through walls like a ghost, and hear and smell things from a great distance."

"And your bosses?" I asked. "What can they do?"

The Smoke made a poor imitation of a shrug in his expensive suit. "I do not know. They are gods, they can do about anything as far as I know."

"And they are working on this as well?" I asked.

"They are," he said.

I nodded, then turned to Patty and Screamer. "Seems we need a God Summit to fix this problem."

"A what?" Screamer asked.

Patty just laughed. "You're not thinking what I think you're thinking, are you?"

I smiled. "I am." Then I turned and shouted into the lilac-smelling air, "Stan!"

CHAPTER THREE

One hour later the four of us, with Stan, were standing in front of Lady Luck's huge oak desk. As best as I could tell from the faint light starting to fill the winter sky over Vegas, her office was floating a few thousand feet in the air. It looked like any other corporate president's office except for the large pair of white dice sitting on the corner of her desk, and the fact that there were windows on all four sides of the room and no building under us.

Lady Luck was dressed in a business power-suit of dark silk, with a white blouse under the vest. Today her hair was brown and pulled back tightly, giving her a serious look that would scare just about anyone, since her features were classic Greek with the sharp, pointed nose and high cheekbones.

I hated standing near or even being around Lady Luck. As a professional poker player, if she got mad at me I could go on a very long and very dry spell of bad cards. Sure, poker was a game of skill, but without a little luck at times, losing would happen much more often.

I had just finished explaining to her what we had found and my suggestion to stop the problem. She was just staring at me with the best poker face I had ever seen.

I just stared back, keeping my own poker face in complete control as well.

"This will take a lot of power to cover the entire continent with a shield like you are suggesting," Laverne said. "I do not have that much power. In fact, all of the gods under my control don't have that kind of power, even for the fraction of a second it will need to be in place."

"I was afraid of that," I said. "But if you combined forces with the animal gods and some of the others, as many others as would be possible, then there might be enough. Right?"

I honestly had no idea if I was correct or not, but I sure hoped I was. Otherwise the world was in for a very tough time with millions of more humans showing up suddenly, all in need of care just as dogs had needed.

I couldn't even imagine just the toilet training issues alone.

She stared at me and then laughed. Having Lady Luck herself laugh at you is not something I had ever imagined happening. Her laugh was sharp and high and it cut.

"You are suggesting something that has never been done before," she said. "All the gods working together. We've never even been in the same time zone or area of the planet at the same time before, let alone work together on anything."

I nodded and said nothing.

Lady Luck walked to the window of her office and stared down at the lights of the Strip below. Then she said "Burt!"

The round, red-faced God of Casino Operations, and second in command of all the gambling universe under Laverne, appeared beside Stan and close to Laverne.

"What do you think of what Poker Boy and his crew are suggesting?" Laverne asked Burt.

"We might get enough of the gods to help if we called in a few chits and asked for a few favors," Burt said. He turned to The Smoke. "What about your bosses?"

"I have already conferred with them and they will follow whatever decision Laverne makes on this. Only a few of them have the power of the shield that will be needed, but they will add what they can."

I didn't say anything, but it was just another example of how Laverne had grown in power over the centuries to become one of the most powerful gods of them all. She only answered to the Fates, and I doubted she even talked to them much these days.

She nodded. "The gods that will help will meet back here in one hour. We have a lot of invitations to send out and little time to do it."

Laverne then nodded to me. "Be prepared to state your case in one hour."

I was about to ask just what she meant by that when the four of us found ourselves back at our normal booth in The Diner.

The front door was still open and the place smelled much better. None of us had drunk our milkshakes, and The Smoke hadn't even gotten his hamburger when we had vanished from the place an hour before. But we had left Madge more than enough money to cover everything before Stan jumped us away to Laverne's office.

"The Weird Bunch is back again," Madge said, coming out from the back room. "What would you like to order this time that you won't eat?"

I was too stunned at what Laverne had said before we jumped back here to even order, so Patty had Madge bring me a vanilla milkshake again. I doubted I would drink it.

What did Lady Luck mean that I needed to be prepared to state my case? After I sat for a moment with that question going over and over through my mind, I turned to Patty.

"What did Laverne mean by 'me stating the case'?"

Patty smiled, but it was the smile I had seen her use on me a number of times when she was humoring me.

Screamer laughed an uneasy laugh. "Laverne is going to pull in as many gods from around the planet as she can and have you explain to them what everyone needs to do."

I opened my mouth, then shut it. I had enough trouble talking to just Stan and Laverne and Burt. How in the world was I going to talk to dozens of different gods all at once? And with so much at stake?

I couldn't do it. I just couldn't. And that meant that very shortly the average IQ of the human race was going to drop dramatically.

Chapter Four

After a half hour of talking with my friends, I was starting to calm down. Finally, with Patty's hand resting on my arm to give me strength, I started to focus on the real problem. If I could get past the stage fright, I had to have an exact plan.

I sipped my vanilla milkshake and then turned to The Smoke. "Do you have the exact frequency needed to change dogs into humans?"

"I do," he said.

"So, are there other frequencies of radiation we need to worry about that change other animals into humans or frogs into cats or things like that?"

He nodded. "There are a few. But the frequency that is due to hit here is exact, and harmless for the most part except for this problem we are facing. All we have to do is block it exactly and we will be fine."

"Better," I said. I turned to the air and shouted "Stan!"

A moment later the restaurant froze with Madge behind the cash register ringing up the money we had given her for our current batch of food and drinks.

"Need a little help," I said to the Poker God now pulling up a chair on the end of the booth. "When you and Burt stopped that explosion at the Bookkeeper's house from spreading anywhere but upward, what kind of field was that? And how did you generate it?"

"You all have one form or another of the same power," Stan said. He looked directly at me. "When you take people out of time, as I have done here now, you simply imagine them slipping between the molecules, right?"

I had to admit he was right. I did it that way. I nodded.

Stan turned to Patty. "When you are working with an upset customer, how do you calm them?"

She nodded. "I change some hormone molecules in their minds to a calming substance that makes them feel good and happy."

Stan turned to The Smoke, who was already nodding. "When I go through walls, I simply imagine the molecules very wide apart so that I can slip through them, like turning the structure of the wall into a gas for an instant."

"Exactly," Stan said, turning back to face me. "All Burt and I did was harden the air around the explosion so nothing could get through for the brief moment of the explosion."

"And that's exactly what we need to do," I said, "for the few seconds the radiation is hitting North America. We need to harden the air enough to block an exact frequency."

"It will work," Stan said. "If we have enough power to generate the hardening field for long enough and at the right time."

"So how many gods are coming to help?" I asked.

Stan stared up at the ceiling for a moment, clearly somewhere else, then said, "Six hundred and twelve."

"There are six hundred and twelve gods?" Screamer asked as I sat back, stunned.

Stan smiled. "Oh, there are far more than that. But only six hundred and twelve have accepted Laverne's invitation to help."

"How in the world is she going to coordinate all of them?" Screamer asked.

"She's not," I said, closing my eyes and trying not to panic. "That's what she wants us to do."

"I'm afraid so," Stan said. "I'll be back in a half hour. She's got a mess with the seating chart that needs all of us working on it. We gods, you know, have egos."

Suddenly the noise of the café and the street outside flooded back in and all I could do was lean back in the booth and try not to panic.

Unsuccessfully.

Chapter Five

After about five minutes, with Patty's gentle touch on my arm, I was calm enough again to work on the problem.

We all four talked for a few minutes, then Screamer said exactly the conclusion I had been coming to. "There's just no way to get over six hundred gods with different levels of powers to cover everywhere completely."

I nodded. "To do that would take years of math and someone like the Bookkeeper to figure it out, and that's if we knew exactly the level of every god's powers. And we don't and never will."

"So how do we do this?" Patty asked. "Are we going to be happy with saving only some dogs and not all?"

I hated that thought. I hated it every time I couldn't save a single dog.

"No," I said, "we need all the power to go through one source and out over the entire continent, to form a complete dome of hardened air for a second or two."

"And who's going to do that?" The Smoke said.

"We are," I said. "All four of us together, linked."

Screamer opened his mouth, then shut it again. Patty just shook her head slowly. The Smoke seemed frozen.

But for the first time in a couple of hours I was starting to feel more confident.

"With the four of us linked, The Smoke can form the dome and make sure we are blocking the right frequency, Screamer can hold us together and add energy, and Patty and I can control and funnel the energy to the shield that The Smoke forms."

"That's going to be a lot of power," Screamer said.

"I don't think we'll survive it," Patty said. "We're not gods."

"And that's why we can do it," I said. "We're the workers, the superheroes who get our hands dirty every day saving lives. We don't need to touch the power, just like a fireman with a powerful hose of water doesn't touch the water. We just aim it."

"I hope you're right, Poker Boy," The Smoke said.

"If I'm not," I said, "we'll be dead and a lot of dogs will be human."

I glanced at the clock on the wall. "We only have a few minutes. We need to practice this a few times."

Screamer nodded for The Smoke to touch his shoulder and then reached for Patty and my hands.

It took us a moment, but then we each settled into our spots in the bigger mind we had created with Screamer's connection.

I thought directly at The Smoke that he should imagine hardening the air over the booth next to ours in a way that would only block a certain frequency.

He did, and then Patty and I formed an imaginary hose and connected it to the shield to power it. We ran through it twice, then Screamer let us go.

"I want to practice that with Stan feeding us some light energy just before we go."

Everyone nodded, so once again I called for Stan.

"Almost time," he said as he appeared, taking us out of time at the same moment.

"One quick practice session," I said. I quickly explained what we were doing. Stan nodded. "Might just work."

For Stan, that was as encouraging as he ever got.

Screamer linked the four of us up and we could hear Stan ask, "Ready?"

"Ready," we said as one, out of four mouths.

He started a slight flow of energy toward us and Patty and I captured it easily into the mouth of the imaginary hose we had formed in our minds and sent it directly to the shield.

Expand the shield, I thought to The Smoke, so that it covers as much as you can with the energy coming to you.

He expanded the shield as Stan increased the energy until

the shield covered all of the Las Vegas area. As more energy came in Patty and I let the natural flow expand the size of the hose protecting all of our minds. It worked easily for one god's worth of energy. Could we hold the containment for over six hundred gods' energy, all directed at the same spot?

If not, we would be four very dead superheroes.

Chapter Six

Stan jumped the four of us back to the front of what looked like a large auditorium floating high over Las Vegas. We were suddenly standing on a stage facing six hundred very powerful gods who stared at us like we were a bad stage act that was bombing.

The colors and styles of clothing in the room seemed to not only cover every possible color in the rainbow, but almost every age of man. I didn't recognize more than one or two of them. I could see the Bookkeeper's bosses, the Gods of Mathematics, in their heavy sweaters and large glasses, but beyond that I had no idea who the rest of the gods were. I was pretty certain I didn't want to know.

Laverne, still dressed in her business suit and white blouse stepped up beside the four of us and started speaking to the crowd. "We have very little time if we are to avert a disaster of epic proportions. We have four superheroes here who need all of our help to solve this problem."

She introduced the four of us and which area of the deities we each worked, then said, "Poker Boy, please tell us how we can help your team solve this problem."

I took a deep breath, dug down deep into the calming poker face and manner that had gotten me through many a stressful tournament, and then with Patty's hand barely touching my arm for support, I explained what we needed and why.

Around the room I could see heads nodding, clearly thinking our plan would work. Others sat perfectly still, expressionless.

When I finished Laverne stepped forward. "I will help focus the power and contain it as it moves through the four of them so that they will not die from the extreme energy being poured through them."

I was very, very happy to hear Laverne say that.

She turned to me again. "Poker Boy, how long will we need to hold the shield?"

"Two seconds," I said, "but it will take a few seconds for us to power up the shield as well, so if the energy can be brought up over the first three seconds, then held for two seconds, it should solve the problem."

Lady Luck nodded, her expression deadly serious, then turned to the audience. "Thank you all for your help. Please be ready."

Burt appeared next to Laverne and said, "Twenty seconds."

"Screamer," I said and he nodded. He stepped between me and Patty and The Smoke moved in behind him. Then The Smoke put both hands on Screamer's shoulder while Patty and I took each of Screamer's hands.

Suddenly we were all together again.

Sure hope this works, the Screamer thought clearly.

Just hold us together no matter what happens, I thought back.

Burt and Laverne stepped in front of us and then turned sideways to the audience facing each other, leaving an opening between them from us to the audience.

"Ten seconds," Burt said.

Screamer's grip on my hand tightened.

Form the hose, I thought at Patty and we formed a very thick, very expandable imaginary hose.

"Five seconds," Burt said.

"Start easy for the first second, then increase the energy," Laverne said to the gods.

Not a sound could be heard in the huge room as every god sat forward, clearly focused on the task at hand.

Every ounce of energy we have to keep this hose together, I thought to Patty. Keep the shield on frequency, I thought at The Smoke.

"Two, one, Now!" Burt said.

The impact of the first energy staggered both Laverne and

Burt, but they both adjusted and the energy hit us, caught by the now seemingly huge imaginary hose in our minds.

Even though Patty and I were focusing all our energy on the hose and holding it in place against the flood of energy, I could see the shield expanding as the energy increased and increased.

Time seemed to slow down as the energy increased. As far as I was concerned, it felt like the hose was the size of a ten-lane interstate and growing, all inside our group minds.

I could feel Patty starting to weaken, so I dug as deep as I could and held. Then I felt her also dig deep and strengthen as well. She was the strongest human I had ever met.

Somehow we held that imaginary hose in our minds together, even as it continued to grow. Just one leak from that stream of energy and we would all be dead. And I wasn't going to allow anything to happen to Patty.

I could sense a thought from The Smoke that the shield was full and holding.

I could feel energy coming from Screamer trying to help me and Patty as much as possible without losing the contact between us he was struggling to hold.

Time stretched and stretched and stretched.

I could feel myself and Patty starting to slip on our hold on the imaginary hose.

The strain was too much.

I couldn't hold this much longer.

It wasn't possible.

It's done! The faint thought came from The Smoke. The radiation is blocked.

"Stop," I said, hoping that was my out-loud voice.

The energy shut off instantly and all four of us slumped to the stage as one.

Screamer let our hands go and I had the sudden feeling of being alone.

Both Lady Luck and Burt staggered backward as well, then worked to catch their breath.

Slowly a sound filled the air and I looked at Patty, who was coming around and looking at me. It took me a moment to realize what the sound was, then I looked out at the mass of gods. They were all standing and applauding.

We were getting a standing ovation from a room full of gods! What a way to start a new year.

And then after a moment the sound stopped and they all vanished, leaving an empty room with only Stan, Laverne, Burt, and the four of us.

Stan helped me to my feet and I helped Patty. Screamer and The Smoke staggered up as well. My knees felt like they were held together by rubber bands, thin ones, but darned if I was going to fall down again in front of Lady Luck, so I braced my legs and Patty leaned against me and we held each other up somehow.

Laverne and Burt both looked tired as well, and there was actually a little sweat on her forehead that vanished after a moment.

Lady Luck actually could sweat. Who knew?

She thanked each of us for the great work, then looked directly at me. "Once again, Poker Boy, you and your team have saved us. All I can say is thank you yet again."

She and Burt vanished, leaving a tired-looking, but smiling Stan, the God of Poker. "How about we all go get something to eat? On me."

"I'm not sure if Madge can handle us three times in one day," I said. "Especially on the first day of the year."

"I was thinking more about the buffet at the MGM Grand. Don't you have some winnings to pick up?"

"I do," I said, smiling, remembering how my year had actually started with my tradition.

Everyone was nodding at the idea so I said, "Perfect. And besides, I wanted to talk to The Smoke here, see if he might be interested in joining us on a few cases down the road?"

The Smoke smiled, again without showing his teeth, then said, "I would be honored." Then he turned to Stan. "I hear the buffet at the MGM Grand has some great meat. Not cooked too much, I hope."

Stan laughed. "You know, you're as weird as the rest of this bunch. You fit perfectly."

"That he does," I said smiling at the werewolf named The Smoke, the newest member of the team.

A moment later the five of us were standing in line for the buffet. Even a god and four superheroes had to stand in line. Even after saving a lot of dogs.

Shootout In The Okey-Doke Casino

Chapter One

In my few, short years working as a superhero for the gambling gods, no one had ever bothered to mention to me that fairies and elves and trolls and all those sorts of things actually existed.

Of course, until I became Poker Boy, I had no idea that just about everything that existed had gods that ruled over that area of the world. Gambling gods, gods of food, gods of hospitality, gods of mathematics, and so on. So I suppose it wasn't much of a jump to realize fairies were real as well. I had just honestly never thought about it.

It was a Monday night, just after nine, and I was playing in a small, two-hundred-dollar buy-in tournament at my local Spirit Winds Casino in the mountains in Oregon. The eleven-table poker room had the three remaining tournament tables tucked off in one corner, with two real-money tables on the other side of the room. I planned on moving to one of the regular tables if I got knocked out of the tournament, and playing until eleven when my girlfriend got off work.

I owned an old double-wide about a half-mile away from the casino, tucked in the back of an old trailer park. I liked playing in the Spirit Winds' small poker room when I wasn't out chasing bad guys or saving dogs – even though I am a superhero in the gambling universe, I seemed to save a lot of dogs. No one could really explain it, beyond it just happened.

I was about to fold a ten-nine-suited to a raise in front of me when someone tapped me on the shoulder.

I glanced around to see Stan, the God of Poker, standing behind me in black slacks, white shirt, and dark sports jacket. No one seemed to notice him.

Actually, Stan was one of the most unnoticeable people I had ever met. His square-jawed face seldom showed emotion and he could disappear completely from just about any crowd without using any superpower at all.

I had on my usual superhero costume of black leather coat, black Fedora-like hat, and jeans. The coat and hat helped focus my powers when I was near or in a casino.

Stan leaned in and said, "Get your team together. Half-hour at The Diner."

Then he turned and headed out the door before I could even ask a question. At the exact spot where there was a three-foot dead spot in camera feeds to security, he vanished.

No doubt something bad was happening. When Stan came in person to Oregon to get me, things were urgent.

I mucked my hand and pushed back from the table, pretending to get a call on my cell phone, the very same phone I never turned on and never used. Then I turned to the dealer after pretending to listen for a moment to a call. "Blind me off. Got to run."

The dealer nodded and a couple of the players actually looked relieved I was leaving.

I waited until I was outside the casino in a blind camera spot before I jumped to another blind camera spot in front of the MGM Grand Hotel and Casino front desk on the Strip in Vegas.

I loved that I knew how to teleport. Teleporting was, at the moment, my favorite superpower. I had just learned how to do it a month or so ago, and it was startling how often it came in handy. Especially when I lived in Oregon and often had to work or rescue people in Las Vegas.

My girlfriend, Patty Ledgerwood, aka Front Desk Girl, is a superhero working under the gods of hospitality. She was standing behind the counter smiling at an overweight woman customer when I arrived in front of the counter beside the customer. I instantly slid Patty and myself out of time, leaving the women who had been trying to register standing with an open mouth full of yellow teeth and eyes half-closed in a blink.

Being able to slip out of time and freeze everything around me was my second-favorite superpower. I had learned how to do that back during the fight with the Slots of Saturn. It never got old.

The noise of the large lobby and the casino down the hall instantly stopped, as did everyone in the lobby except Patty and me.

"Knocked out of the tournament already?" Patty asked, smiling and reaching across the wide counter to take my hand and give it an affectionate squeeze.

Her big brown eyes and wonderful smile could melt an iceberg, and every time she turned that smile and that wonderful gaze on me, I melted right along with the berg. She had her long brown hair pulled back and had on the standard white blouse and black slacks of the MGM front desk, where she worked.

"Stan came and got me," I said. "We have some sort of mission. He didn't say what kind, but it sounded urgent."

She nodded, reached into her pocket, and slid me her cell phone, knowing mine was only a prop. "It will take me a minute to finish with this customer," she said, indicating the open-mouthed woman who really, really needed a dentist. "Then I'll be ready to go. Give Screamer a call."

"Is The Smoke in town?"

"No," she said. "Off working a case of bear-killings in Alaska."

I slipped us back into real time as I turned and walked away from the counter. The noise of all the people and tourists talking at the same time as I crossed the stone and high-ceilinged room rammed into me again.

I dialed Screamer's number and then stood against a stone pillar to stay out of the traffic lane.

"So what's up?" Screamer asked.

"Stan called us together," I said. "You free in a half hour?"

"I'm out at the airport," he said. "Got about fifteen minutes to finish the case here with airport security."

"Call when you are done and I'll jump you to The Diner."

"Got it," he said and hung up.

Screamer worked as a superhero for the gods of law enforcement. His main power was being able to crawl inside a person's head, and transfer thoughts from one person to another. It came in very handy in more ways than can be imagined.

He got his nickname when he got a serial killer to scream for mercy by letting him experience what he had put others through. Screamer got the guy to tell the police where he had buried a woman alive and the police got there in time to save the woman.

It took the killer an hour to stop screaming from whatever Screamer had put in his head.

The fourth member of our team was The Smoke, a werewolf who had complete control over which form he was in and who could also walk through walls. He worked as a superhero for the animal gods.

Our team was the only team I knew about that crossed over four areas of gods, and we had done our share of saving humanity since we formed.

I sure hoped the mission tonight was a more mundane one, but with Stan coming to get me, that wasn't likely.

Patty vanished into the back area behind the counter. About one minute later she came out into the lobby, headed for me.

She kissed me, then hand-in-hand we turned and headed for the parking garage.

"We got time to drive?" Patty asked as we started down the staircase.

"Yeah," I said. "Stan said thirty minutes, it's only been less than fifteen."

So we got to The Diner in downtown Las Vegas the old-fashioned way. We drove.

Chapter Two

The Diner was a small hole-in-the-wall restaurant downtown on a side street about a half-block from the Horseshoe Casino. It had fantastic milkshakes that almost matched its fake 1960s décor. And Madge, the waitress, ran the place. She was a superhero working for the gods of food and beverage, and she didn't mind us jumping in and out as long as her other customers didn't notice.

Madge was a large woman in many ways, and always wore a uniform two sizes too small for her build, which meant watching her walk away in her tight skirt wasn't something anyone wanted to do.

Just like my black leather coat and hat was my uniform and gave me extra power, her tight skirt and too-tight white blouse was clearly hers. Not sure what powers it gave her, or if those powers were worth it, to be honest.

"Been a week," Madge said as Patty and I walked in the door, "since the last time you guys saved the world. I figure, since you are walking this time, whatever is going on now can't be that important."

"Nice seeing you as well, Madge," I said, smiling at her as she popped her gum.

"Who else is joining you lovebirds?" she asked as we took our normal booth. Patty and I slid in beside each other leaving the other side open for Screamer. No one else was in the place and Madge looked almost happy to see us.

"Screamer and Stan," Patty said. "Milkshakes."

Madge nodded. "Let me know if there's anything I can do to help you guys this time around. What you did for all those dogs a while back was really special."

"Thanks," I said.

She turned away to go make milkshakes as Stan appeared.

"Where is everyone?" he asked, looking worried as he pulled up a chair in front of the booth.

"Screamer is finishing up at the airport and needs a jump here when he's done. The Smoke is in Alaska on another case."

"The moose-shooting thing by the ex-governor," Stan said, nodding.

"Bear," Patty corrected.

Stan nodded again. "He might need some help on that when we finish with this one."

At that moment, Patty's cell phone buzzed and she took it out of her pocket and glanced at it. "Screamer," she said.

Before I could jump to get him and bring him back, Screamer was sitting across from Patty and me, his cell phone still to his ear.

"Thanks, Stan," he said, snapping the phone closed and putting it in his dark shirt pocket.

Stan hadn't left the table. Looks like I had a lot more to learn about teleporting – I didn't know that stunt was even possible.

"So what's happening?" Patty asked Stan as she put her phone away.

"The fairies have challenged the trolls again," Stan said.

Patty suddenly looked worried. "The Curse of the Bayback Bridge."

"I thought we had another twenty years before that hit," Screamer said.

"We all did," Stan said, the look of seriousness on his face making my stomach twist. "But someone rebuilt the bridge damned fast this time around."

Well, I knew that was all in English, but just because Stan said it like I should understand it didn't mean I did.

But Patty clearly did.

And so did Screamer.

Sometimes being the new kid in the superhero neighborhood just sucked. I knew Patty was a good hundred years older than I was, and I had never asked Screamer how long he had been around. Stan remembered Atlantis, and once mentioned he had been born there.

Me, I was born in 1950, and sort of stopped aging around

thirty-five when I got hired as a superhero by the gambling gods. I had been told I wouldn't age for a very long time, which I honestly liked the sound of. But having a girlfriend a hundred years older than I was sometimes felt just intimidating.

"What are they fighting about this time?" Screamer asked, shaking his head.

"Is this normal," I asked, afraid to mention I didn't know who the trolls or the fairies were. Or what the "Curse of the Bayback Bridge" even was. At that moment, it hadn't occurred to me they were talking about kids' books trolls and fairies. I thought they meant some sort of teenage gangs or something.

"About every thirty to fifty years," Stan said, "the curse makes them fight again. This time it seems the fight is over which group is a better no-limit poker player."

"You're kidding?" Patty asked, almost laughing.

"I wish I was," Stan said. "And it's up to us to make sure the tournament they are staging is settled and doesn't explode into a bigger battle. Direct orders from all our bosses while they find and blow up that damned bridge again. Our job is to control the fight and make sure it's fair if they can't find the bridge before the tournament starts."

"Fair with trolls' dark magic and fairy fancy magic?" Screamer asked, shaking his head. "Now that's going to be a real trick."

"There is no magic in poker," I said, still not having a clue what I was really talking about.

"Exactly," Stan said. "So we have to figure out a way to keep magic out of this tournament completely. And we have two hours until it starts."

"What starts?" Madge said as she arrived with our milkshakes.

"The trolls and fairies are fighting again, in a poker tournament this time," Stan said, pulling his chocolate milkshake closer to him.

"The curse again?" Madge asked, clearly disgusted. "Count me out of this one. Two or three battles back those ugly, smelly, little trolls trashed my restaurant in a food fight against the fairies. I'm afraid if I see any of them again they may get even shorter."

With that she walked off.

Both Stan and Screamer were laughing.

"Okay, I admit," I said, "I'm the baby here, so I'm going to need a little help. What exactly are trolls and fairies?"

All three of them were starting to sip on their milkshakes and all three stopped and looked at me like I had lost my mind, which I was starting to think I might be doing.

"You ever read any fairytales when you were a kid?" Screamer asked.

It finally, at that moment, dawned on me. "You're telling me that *fairies* and *trolls* are real?"

"Yeah," Screamer said, laughing.

Patty patted my hand and pushed my milkshake closer to me.

"Very real," Stan said. "And don't believe that Tinker-Bell

fairy stuff the movies show. Real fairies are tall, skinny, and pranksters. Mean pranksters. And the trolls are short, but not that short. They tend to smell like two-day-old fish, and they are naturally as rude as an angry landlord. But they don't live under things. In fact a lot of them in this area live in a big condo complex out by the university."

"And some of them are married to fairies," Patty said.

I took a deep breath and tried to let all that sink in. Then, after a wonderful, cool sip of my vanilla milkshake, I asked the next question. "What is this curse, and why is their poker tournament so important, and why do we care that the trolls and fairies are fighting?"

I guess that was three questions, but shoot me. I was confused.

"Far before I was born," Stan said, "a God of Domestic Happiness named Roger Bayback got into a really nasty divorce from his fairy wife after she had an affair with a troll. He put a dark magic curse on all fairies and trolls. The curse actually flows from the bridge his wife and the troll had sex under. As long as the bridge stands, the two races must fight."

"You remember reading about World War Two?" Screamer asked.

I nodded.

"Hitler was a troll," Stan said. "He took over Germany after the bridge was rebuilt. It's been destroyed many times over the centuries, and he did everything in his power to clear out all fairies. And he did his kind and fairy-kind deep harm."

"Not counting what he did to everyone else," I said.

All three nodded at that and Stan went on. "Hitler's attitude was that if he killed everything and everyone in Europe who might be a fairy, eventually he'd get them all."

"Thankfully, he failed," Screamer said.

"But because of that," Stan said, "all the gods stepped in and destroyed the bridge. And we keep destroying it every time it rebuilds in a new location. And we brokered a long-term peace between the fairies and the trolls."

"But since the fairies and the trolls must fight whenever the bridge is up, because of the curse," Screamer said, "part of the truce is that the fighting be in a contained way, like a poker tournament."

"So we have to figure out a way to stop both their magic, and just let them play poker?" I asked, "Or it might escalate into something much bigger?"

"Exactly," Stan said.

"Why don't the gods just break the curse forever?"

Stan shook his head. "Can't do that unless we can find Roger Bayback, and he has been missing for thousands and thousands of years."

"So how are we going to contain both fairy *and* troll magic so they can just play poker?" Screamer asked.

I just stared at my milkshake, trying to wrap my mind around fairies and trolls being real. Let alone some ancient curse on them.

Stan shrugged. "That's what we have less than two hours to figure out if the gods can't find that damn bridge."

No one said a word.

The image of Hitler as a troll just kept flashing through my mind. Not an image I wanted to keep.

Chapter Three

A half-hour later, after Stan and Patty explained troll and fairy magic to me, I knew there was no chance that this coming tournament would even last through the first fifteen minute round.

Alone, without magic and curses and other fairytale issues, poker was a game of emotions and frustration and cold, hard calculations. The first bad beat put on a troll by a fairy would send the room into full-fledged war, magic or no magic, curse or no curse.

"Whose idea was it to fight in a poker tournament?" I asked. "Anyone who knows poker knows that it's a guaranteed way to escalate a fight instead of contain it. Even blocking or taking away all the player's magic won't matter in the slightest."

"I said the same thing to Laverne," Stan said. "But it was

decided that a poker tournament was the form of combat this time, unless the bridge can be found first."

Laverne was Lady Luck herself, one of the most powerful of all gods.

Something was really bothering me that I couldn't put my finger on. This staged fighting thing had been going on since after the Second World War.

"Who decided that?" I asked. "Who suggested a poker tournament?"

Stan stared at me for a moment, then said simply, "I'll find out."

He vanished and then came back less than ten seconds later.

"The poker room manager at the Okey-Doke suggested it," Stan said.

I think I just stared blankly at him.

He laughed when he saw my look and said, "The Okey-Doke Casino and Hotel is where all the fairy-folk gamble. It's magically hidden from real people. It's out on the old highway headed toward the dam."

That wasn't why I was looking blank. I couldn't understand why a poker room manager had suggested the battle? Poker room managers know how impossible it can be at times to keep even normal human poker players under control, let alone races with magic forced to fight under a curse. Again, nothing about this was making sense.

I sat back for a moment and just stared at the ceiling, trying to ignore all the stuff I didn't understand, or had just learned. Instead I tried to make sense of all this from a very human viewpoint.

Point one: An angry ex-husband wanted to take out revenge on his ex-wife and her new lover's peoples. Okay, a little over-the-top, but understandable, considering the sex under a bridge part.

Point two: If I was the very screwed-up angry husband, I would want to watch every battle to get my emotional satisfaction.

Suddenly I had an idea.

"What does this Roger Bayback look like?" I asked.

"No one really knows anymore," Stan said. "This is a very old curse. And besides, he's a god, he can disguise himself completely."

I nodded. I had a hunch I knew exactly where Roger Bayback was, but I didn't dare trust my instincts alone, so I turned to Stan.

"If we have to fight this battle, here's how you set up the tournament. Two brackets, equal number of players in both. Equal chips. Trolls only in one bracket, fairies only in the other bracket. Winner of both brackets face off in a showdown. One on one. That should keep the chance of violence down."

Stan nodded. "Great idea."

He started to move, but I stopped him before he jumped. "Tell Laverne and Patty's boss and a number of other gods to watch me carefully, then jump me and Patty and Screamer to the Okey-Doke poker room and support us."

Stan looked as confused as Screamer and Patty looked.

"I have a hunch I know where Roger is, and if I'm right, it's going to take a bunch of gods to contain him."

Stan, still puzzled, nodded and vanished.

If anyone could contain this Roger-god, it was Lady Luck.

I turned to Screamer and Patty. "We might need to be hooked up, Screamer, if I am wrong on my first guess of who Roger is."

"Hooking up" was when Screamer touched us both at the same time so all three of us could be connected and acting as fast as we could think.

"Why?" Patty asked.

"We're going to need to quickly screen a lot of bystanders," I said.

"Laverne and everyone is ready," Stan said, appearing again on his chair.

"If my first ploy doesn't work," I said to Stan, "we're going to need to take a large number of people in a large area around the tournament set-up out of time. If Roger is in area, will he know he's been taken out of time?"

"Yes," Stan said. "But by jumping out of a time bubble like that, he can be traced."

"Okay, then if he's not in that area, Screamer, we go to the second back-up plan. You and Patty and I are going to need to be linked to check everyone close by to see if we can spot in their minds where this poker idea was planted and by who."

"Still confused on plan one and the *first* back-up plan," Stan said.

"You'll see plan one when we get there," I said. "If that fails, the back-up plan is to trap him and make him jump."

"Got you," Stan said. "But why do you think he's there?"

"If you were as pissed-off as he has been for thousands of years, wouldn't you be there to watch the bloodshed?"

Stan and Patty and Screamer all nodded slowly.

For an instant Stan seemed to look up, then he was back in his eyes. "Laverne and the rest are ready."

"Then let's go," I said.

Chapter Four

Stan jumped us right into the front area of a large poker room that held a good thirty tables. Around the rail a large group of faintly-blue fairies stood in a group, talking. They were tall and thin and laughed a lot among themselves.

Not a one of them had wings that I could see. Not sure why I expected wings, but I did.

I stared for a minute, still working to get past my shock that fairies were real. Then I looked around to the other side of the room to a group of trolls, trying to get the image of Hitler out of my mind but failing. They all looked like fire-plugs with human bodies and greasy black hair.

At first glance, The Okey-Doke Casino and Hotel seemed very much like any other casino in Vegas, except for the unicorns carrying drinks between slot machines on their backs, and the giant ponds and streams that wound through a huge forest, dividing the blackjack tables from the slots and making the entire thing look like it was a casino parked in an ancient forest. Even the carpets looked like pine needles.

And the place smelled like no other casino I had ever been in. No cigarette smoke, but a distinct odor of sour milk.

All my warning superpowers went into high gear. This was not a friendly place for most humans or superheroes. But after studying the place for a moment, I suddenly had a back-up plan three.

I nodded to Stan and then walked toward the poker room counter. It looked again like any other main counter in any poker room, with sign-up whiteboards behind it on the wall showing all the tables and possible games. Right now all the boards were wiped clean as everyone got ready for the tournament.

I walked up to the guy who was clearly the poker room manager. He was short, but human, with gray hair and a long gray beard that made him look more Gandalf-like instead of a poker room manager. He had on a white shirt, with a green vest over it, and black pants. That was the traditional uniform of most dealers and brushes that worked poker rooms.

"I'm Poker Boy," I said, coming up beside him as he stacked racks of blue and red tournament chips on a table. I motioned at the other three of my team behind me. "We're here to help keep the tournament under control."

"Great to have you," the guy said, not looking up. "We should be ready to go in about fifteen minutes."

"Great," I said. "We'll be over by the rail."

He nodded and kept counting. I turned and started to walk away, then winked at my team and turned back.

"Oh, Roger, one more thing."

He looked up without thinking. Then I could see in his eyes he understood what I had done.

An instant later he froze in place, solid as a rock, before he could even think of jumping. In fact, he looked like he had actually become rock, like a carved Greek statue holding a rack of poker chips.

Lady Luck appeared, wearing a power suit of black silk with silver stripes. She was smiling, staring at the rock that had been the god, Roger Bayback.

After a moment she turned to all of us. "We finally got this guy. Great job, Poker Boy. Everyone. Now we just have to find that stupid bridge one last time."

I pointed to the middle of the casino. A short bridge, styled like an ancient European bridge, crossed over a large pond to a high-stakes slot area. She turned and saw what I was pointing at, then just shook her head.

A moment later the bridge was gone in a cloud of smoke, stranding a bunch of elfin-looking old women on the island of high-stakes.

The Curse of the Bayback Bridge was gone forever.

"You don't know how many lives you might have just saved," Laverne said, smiling at me. "Thank you and your team once again."

Every time Lady Luck had smiled at me, I got chills, and

this time was no exception. I was a poker player, after all. You didn't take something like that lightly.

With a slight nod to all of us, she and the now-stone-god vanished to cheers from all the fairies and trolls standing around watching.

The cheers and celebration was so loud that I couldn't even hear the bells on the slot machines.

Trolls were kissing trolls.

Fairies were kissing fairies.

And trolls and fairies were kissing each other.

Now every warning power in my body was off, and I could feel this wonderful feeling of welcome and warmth.

It looked like the poker tournament had just been cancelled. And I had to admit, this was the first time I had been happy about a tournament cancellation.

Stan smiled, looking around. "Poker Boy, it seems you have a new room you are welcome to play in."

I glanced around at all the laughing and cheering and dancing fairies and trolls. "Thanks, but no thanks. I have a hard enough time reading human faces."

What I didn't say was that I just couldn't shake the image of Hitler as a troll.

A moment later the four of us were back in The Diner.

And this time the burgers and fries and milkshakes were paid for by Lady Luck.

Pink Shoes And Hot Chocolate

CHAPTER ONE

When you're a superhero, you don't often notice pink women's shoes. I'm usually far too busy saving the world from evil, saving dogs from sure death, or playing professional poker, my day job that pays the bills of being a superhero. Pink shoes rarely come into the picture. In fact, I have no memory of ever thinking about pink shoes before.

Yet there sat a pair of bright pink dress shoes with very long heals on the small pile of brown sand six miles outside of Las Vegas.

The wind was blowing through the sagebrush and rocks and I was having trouble keeping my black, Fedora-like poker hat on my head. The hat was part of my superhero costume, along with my black leather jacket. With the hat and jacket on and a casino nearby, I had more powers than I have had time to explore. Sometimes my powers even surprise me.

But out in the desert, with the wind threatening to take my hat and make me chase it like a playful dog through the rocks, I didn't feel very powerful. And the pair of women's pink shoes sitting on the mound didn't help the issue.

Around me, the very early morning sun was heating up the desert to the point that shortly it would be far too warm for me to wear my black leather jacket even with a wind. The heat was the reason I had headed out of town at five in the morning. I never saw five in the morning normally, except from the night side. Getting up at this frightful hour showed how much I cared about this case. It had taken me only an hour to find the shoes, since I had a hunch exactly where to look.

The pink shoes belonged to Carol Savage, a thin, athletic Keno runner at the Atlantis Hotel and Casino. Carol stood two inches taller than my six-foot height and she was much, much thinner. Not that I'm fat. I'm not. Carol is just thin.

Carol had a smile that could light up a room and her dark green eyes seemed to laugh at everything. I figured she had to have a great life attitude, being a Keno runner. The old joke around the poker world was that Keno was for gamblers who had lost the will to live. Carol radiated life like the sun gave off light. She was a joy to be around, always.

Bernice, the God of Keno, hated that old joke, but of all the Gambling Gods, she was the lowest ranked and only had one superhero like me working under her. That was Carol, also known as SK (Super Keno) to the rest of the Gambling Gods and all the superheroes who worked for them.

Everyone liked SK; Bernice we could all do without.

When Carol went missing, I got the first call to help find her. Every one of the Gambling Gods seemed to know that she and I had been an item five or six years back, working a couple of cases together. That was before I met Front Desk Girl.

I am known as Poker Boy, one of a dozen poker super-heroes working under Stan, the God of Poker.

And, of course, we all worked under Laverne, Lady Luck herself. And when Laverne asked Stan to have me search for Carol, what was I going to say? Hell, you don't turn down Lady Luck if you ever wanted to win another hand of cards.

With one hand I held my hat on my head and with the other I picked up Carol's pink shoes and studied them. Nothing unusual. She had simply kicked them off and put them on the sand.

I had seen no sign of Carol's car along the road, or any car parked close by, so either she had hidden it in the desert some-where or someone had dropped her off here.

I placed the pink shoes back exactly where Carol had left them and studied the flat desert around me, squinting my eyes and trying to draw on what superpowers I had remaining this far from a casino. It wasn't much, I do have to admit, like a car trying to run on three of six cylinders. I sputtered a lot, but finally found what I was looking for.

There, in plain sight, yet hidden so any normal mortal

would never see it, was the opening to the Silicon Suckers city. I had no idea why Carol hadn't used the main entrance under the Hilton Billboard on Highway 95, but she must have had her reasons. I knew the desert was scattered with entrances to the Silicon Sucker's city, but I had only found one other besides the main entrance and this one.

Silicon Suckers were a race of intelligent creatures that had lived on Earth far, far longer than mankind. They were secretive and shy at best, and almost impossible to see if they didn't want to be seen. They inhabited the major deserts of the world, living in cities underground.

Legends of aliens visiting Earth had come about from sightings of Silicon Suckers. They were commonly called The Grays by UFO nuts. They had large heads, large eyes, no chins, and flat ears. Their arms and legs were thinner than Carol's and they seldom wore clothes. Even without clothes, I couldn't tell the difference between a female and a male Silicon Sucker, although I was told that the difference was clear if you knew what you were looking for.

With humans I knew. Not a clue with Silicon Suckers and I had no great desire to look.

The Silicon Suckers were a highly ritualized race, and the best way to get on their bad side was to violate one of their customs. Wearing shoes in their city was a major violation. Not bringing them a gift they would like when visiting was another. I had a small thermos of hot chocolate in my jacket pocket as my gift to them. Hot chocolate, for some reason or another, was a major delicacy for them. A thermos-full would be shared by the drop among thousands.

I once watched a Silicon Sucker put a drop of hot chocolate on his snake-like tongue and then just stand there, huge eyes closed, swaying back and forth humming something that sounded a lot like our National Anthem played very, very slowly.

Whatever the Silicon Sucker experienced with the hot chocolate was clearly something I could only imagine, since I didn't drink and have never taken drugs of any kind.

I just hoped Carol had known enough about the Suckers to bring them something good. I had a hunch, though, she had done something very, very wrong, since after three days missing, her shoes were still here.

Just in case I needed to buy her way out, I had two other thermoses full of hot chocolate in pockets inside my coat.

I took a deep breath, kicked off my old Nike tennis shoes and left them beside Carol's pink shoes, then headed for the opening between the two rocks. I had been inside the Silicon Sucker's city near Las Vegas three times over my years as a superhero, and it always made me uncomfortable and itchy. The last time I had been trying to save the life of an old college girlfriend who had been given new breast implants made from the sand of a sacred Silicon Suckers burial site

The Suckers wanted their dead ancestors back; my old girlfriend wasn't willing to give them back, no matter how much I pleaded or offered to pay for another operation. She was found dead a month later. I seldom like to think how she died, since the myth about alien probes have a basis in the Silicon Suckers' belief that the only way inside a human body is through the anus.

Those were very large breasts she had. It had to have been painful.

Chapter Two

I had no idea what case Carol had been working for the Gambling Gods to take her to a Silicon Suckers city. But Stan had told me to look here first, and I had found her shoes at the second entrance I checked.

I stopped at the entrance to the city, bowed once exactly as prescribed for any visitor to the city, and then stepped through the slight magic spell that hid the entrance from normal humans.

Inside the dry, brown cave, two Silicon Suckers bowed in return and then indicated I should follow them.

My nose was assaulted by the smell of sand and an intense dryness to the air. My skin felt suddenly tight as if the air was trying to suck every ounce of moisture from my body.

Actually, it was.

They led me down toward the city in what looked like nothing more than a cave carved out of the desert sand and rock. It was lit faintly by soft lights hidden along the ceiling. The more we walked, the raspier my throat felt. It had happened every time to me, but no water was allowed in their cities, so I hadn't dared bring anything to help with the dryness and intense thirst that would soon hit me.

And drinking any of the hot chocolate I had with me while in their city was considered a terminal offence.

I worried a lot about Carol being able to survive three days without water in this environment. I know I would have a hard time.

It wasn't until we had walked downward for almost a half hour that we finally emerged into the vast central chamber of the Silicon Suckers city.

The first time I had seen the massive city with the teaming thousands of Suckers moving about their daily lives, I had been stunned. This time was no different.

Towers of sand-colored round buildings shot from the cavern floor at least thirty stories into the air, elevated walkways spanned the open spaces between the buildings, and the entire cavern hummed with a distant ocean sound that I had been told was nothing more than the sound of a lot of Silicon Suckers moving around at once.

The cavern was lit by an intense, sun-like light, right in the middle and thousands of other lights on the buildings and along the wide streets. No carriages or any type of transportation moved inside the city. Silicon Suckers walked everywhere they went.

And the huge chamber felt even drier than the tunnels, if that was possible. It smelled of lightly burned wood, and I found myself blinking a lot more than normal to keep some hint of moisture in my eyes.

Thousands and thousands of openings went into the dirt all the way around the cavern. We had come out of one such opening about twenty stories in the air, and immediately started down a fairly wide path along the wall.

There was no guardrail on the edge of the path, so I stayed to the inside, hugging the wall. I might be a superhero in the gambling world, but I was fairly certain that none of my superpowers included flying. Flying just didn't seem to be of much use at a poker table.

Without ever asking me what I wanted or who I wanted to see, my two guides led me down to the ground level of the city, then into a building that had to be twenty stories tall and was fairly close to the center of the city. I couldn't tell one tall, brown tower from another, but for some reason this one felt special to me.

Inside they lead me into another tunnel that continued down for another two or three stories, finally opening into a large chamber with four Silicon Suckers sitting cross-legged in the middle of the floor in a circle.

Carol sat cross-legged with them, nodding at something.

She glanced up and saw me, then burst into a huge smile that must have hurt her extremely chapped and dry lips.

"Poker Boy," she said without standing. "Thanks for coming."

"Laverne sent me," I said, moving toward the circle.

"I know," Carol said, a twinkle in her eyes.

I had no idea how she could know that. But asking at that moment just seemed very, very wrong.

Chapter Three

One of my guides indicated that I should sit in the open spot in the circle beside Carol facing the four Silicon Suckers.

Even though I wanted to hug or even lightly touch Carol to tell her I was glad to see her, I knew something simple as a touch between humans in a Silicon Sucker city would a very bad breach of protocol, and since I had no idea what was going on or what part I was to play, I was very careful to not sit too near Carol.

After taking my position, I reached into my front pocket and pulled out a thermos of hot chocolate.

In my best Silicon Sucker click and wheep and stutter, I said, "A gift to thank you for the honor of visiting your wonderful city."

At least I hope that was what I said.

I sat the thermos down and placed my hands in my lap, bowing my head in just the right manor to show respect.

"We accept your wonderful gift to our people. Welcome again, Poker Boy. You are always an honored member of our city."

The Silicon Sucker who spoke didn't move his tiny lips and I wasn't sure if I heard his words with my ears or inside my head. Didn't matter, at least he spoke in English and I didn't have to attempt his language any more.

I nodded my thank you, as prescribed, but said nothing more.

"May we resume our discussions?" Carol asked, her words sounding hoarse from so much exposure to the dry air.

I had no idea how, if she had been down here for three days, she was even managing to sit and talk. Her strength stunned me, but clearly it was wearing on her. Even a super-hero like her had limits.

The Silicon Sucker on the right nodded and in the middle of the circle, floating in the air, a map appeared, shimmering and see-through.

It took me a moment to realize exactly what I was looking at. The Silicon Suckers city was colored in gold on the map, their sacred burial grounds in gold, as well as large acres of other ground I had no idea what they used it for. Highway 95 on one side marked one border and the edge of the city of Las Vegas was a black area on the map.

It seemed that a tiny area just off Highway 95 was in question, as it was blinking between gold and black. When I realized the scale of the map, that tiny area suddenly became larger than a hundred acres.

"I am sure we can come to a fair exchange for the land in question," Carol said, nodding her respect as she spoke. "Poker Boy has brought the first of our many payments to you."

Carol nodded to me and I stared at her for a moment, wondering for a second just exactly what she was talking about. Then I remembered the two other thermoses of hot chocolate I had inside my coat.

I took out one and placed it carefully beside the first, bowing with respect as I did, then placed the third beside the other two.

I had no idea what to say at such a moment, and as I had learned over the years in both poker and doing superhero deeds, if you aren't sure exactly what to say, say nothing.

But damned if I didn't want to ask Carol how she knew I would bring those extra two thermoses with me.

Carol bowed slightly to the Silicon Suckers. "Only the first of many payments to come in exchange for the use of your very valuable land."

"May we understand, please, that your people will bring us every full moon cycle, ten such containers of the precious fluid?"

Carol nodded. "That is my understanding, yes."

I almost snorted, which would have been a huge breach in protocol and more than likely an insult in the Silicon Suckers language. I couldn't believe that Carol was trading what looked like a good one hundred acres of land near Highway 95 for basically ten large mugs of hot chocolate per month. I knew land prices were down, but that was ridiculous.

Chapter Four

"It is agreed," the Silicon Sucker said. The parcel on the map that had been going between gold and black turned black and stayed black.

"It is agreed," Carol said.

The map vanished and the four Silicon Suckers stood and turned away, moving toward an opening in the brown sand wall.

Carol struggled to her feet and stood, clearly exhausted and dehydrated. She needed to get to the hospital and get there quickly, but there was no way I could dare touch her to help her until we cleared that entrance a good fifty stories over our heads.

Our two guides appeared and nodded that we should follow them. I stepped in behind Carol and we headed upward through what I thought was the same tunnel we had come down.

For the first hundred or so steps, Carol staggered, and I was afraid she was going to fall, then she seemed to gain some inner strength and her back straightened, her head came up, and she looked straight ahead as if walking the floor selling Keno tickets.

She was one strong lady.

Back at the surface, we both bowed to our guides and stepped through into the extreme temperatures of the desert in the middle of the afternoon. It had to be well over one hundred and the dry wind hit us both like a hammer.

Carol walked ten steps and then went down, face-first, right on her pink shoes.

The hot wind battered at my hat as I knelt beside her. She was out completely, and from the looks of her in the light, she was on the verge of dying from dehydration.

I snapped open my cell phone and called 911, telling them where along the highway to have an ambulance meet me, then I called my girlfriend and sidekick, Patty Ledgerwood, a.k.a. Front Desk Girl, and told her to find Stan and tell him I was coming in with SK and to get our people at the hospital ready.

I carried the thin Keno-runner superhero to my rental car and laid her out on the back seat. She weighed almost nothing and that scared me a lot. She couldn't die for a piece of property. That just seemed too stupid. I had almost died a number of times trying to rescue a person, but never for a real estate sale, especially in a bad market.

Chapter Five

I met the ambulance at the corner I had indicated, and they worked on her for a good fifteen minutes, getting fluid into her system and checking her vitals before loading her into the ambulance and rushing to the hospital, lights and sirens blaring, with me right on their tail.

By the time I had parked and gotten into the emergency room, she was out of sight. Patty, Stan, and Bernice were all in the waiting room looking worried.

"Good job getting her out of there," Stan said. "Did she get the deal done?"

"She did," I said, staring at Stan, surprised. "You knew what she was doing in there?"

"Not until Bernice told me," Stan said, clearly disgusted, "after you had left."

I stared at Bernice, a short stubby little God that I didn't much like and had even less respect for. "You want to tell me why you risked Carol's life on a property deal with the Silicon Suckers?"

"Huge new Bingo and Keno parlor is planned for that ground along with a large retirement home. The county wouldn't agree, of course, since the Gods blocked building on any of the Silicon Suckers' ground. It was the only way to get the approval."

"And that was worth Carol's life?"

"Of course not," Bernice snapped. "That's why we sent you in to rescue her. The negotiations were only supposed to take a day and we didn't expect her to succeed. We knew things had gone wrong when she hadn't come out in two days."

I gave the short little Keno God my most intense poker stare until she turned away and started pacing.

Stan patted me on the shoulder. "Laverne's in there with her. Carol will make it."

Patty slipped her hand into mine and I could feel the calming influence she had over me. Her super powers concerned making people happy, among other things, and she could calm me down with a touch.

She pulled me over to a row of black, plastic chairs along one wall and we sat down. She handed me a bottle of water and I downed it quickly. Never had water tasted so good.

She handed me another after I finished the first bottle, then said, "So, you want to tell me what happened to your shoes?"

I glanced down at my feet and the very dirty white socks I still wore. "They are beside Carols' pink dress shoes, at the entrance to the Silicon Suckers city. Can't wear shoes down there."

Over the next half hour I told her and Stan and Bernice exactly what had happened and what Carol had managed to do, including the long walk back to the surface on her own.

Just as I finished, Laverne, Lady Luck herself, walked out of the back of the emergency room area and nodded. "She's going to make it. She's asleep and can have visitors tomorrow."

"Oh, thank you," Bernice said, slumping in her chair.

"Nice job once again, Poker Boy," Laverne said. I could only smile. When Lady Luck herself thanked you, there just wasn't much to say.

Patty squeezed my hand.

"We have to talk," Laverne said, staring at Bernice.

They both vanished.

"Good job, kid," Stan said and vanished as well.

Patty helped me to my feet and we headed toward the door. Outside, in the heat, I really noticed that I didn't have shoes as I moved from one shaded area to the next across the hot pavement.

As we got settled in my car, Patty turned to me. "I still don't get the hot chocolate part of all this."

"Think drugs," I said. "Hot chocolate is their most valuable drug."

"So how did you know to take extra hot chocolate, and how did Carol know you were bringing it?"

"You want my guess?" I asked and Front Desk Girl nodded.

"Carol knew that I would be the one the Gods picked to try to find her, since I knew her and had dealings in the past with the Silicon Suckers."

"Got that," Patty said.

"And after being down there for three days, Carol knew I would bring the only real thing of value to a Silicon Sucker to buy her freedom, so she used it as a lure in the purchase instead of a bribe for her release."

"That could have gone so very wrong," Front Desk Girl said.

"Carol knows me, and clearly knew who she was negotiating with. Something must have happened to force her to stay that long and take such a huge risk. We won't know exactly what went wrong until tomorrow."

Front Desk Girl shook her head. "Hot chocolate as a drug. Who would have thought?"

"I can understand that on a cold winter night in front of a crackling fire."

"I thought I was your drug of choice," she said, laughing and rubbing her hand along my leg, sending happy feelings throughout my tired body.

"Oh, you are, you are."

She looked at me with a smile that could melt any angry customer standing at a front desk, let alone a tired poker player. "How about we go back to my place and I'll get you a couple more bottles of water and help you scrub off some of that sand and dirt in a nice cool shower?"

"Perfect," I said. "But first, can we go get my shoes and Carol's shoes from the desert?"

"Sure, but why? I've seen your shoes and they aren't worth the gas out there."

"Not for mine, for Carol's shoes," I said. "In all my years of being a superhero, I've never rescued pink shoes before."

Patty laughed. "I guess there's a first time for everything."

THE ATLANTIS FIFTY

CHAPTER ONE

I got stuck in an instant of time on Saturday afternoon at 12:37 and seven seconds, exactly.

Actually, I woke up stuck.

I knew something was very wrong the instant I woke up. Not only was my warning voice telling me something was wrong, but the sounds were gone from the Las Vegas Strip that normally filled the background of Patty's apartment like a faint sound of the ocean when you stay near the beach.

I could hear nothing.

Either I had gone deaf while sleeping, or something else was going on.

I tapped the bed stand with my alarm clock and heard the sound of my knuckle on the fine oak just fine.

Nope. Not deaf.

Patty wasn't in bed beside me, but I figured she hadn't

been up long. We had both been up until after four in the morning last night, her working until three at the MGM Grand and me playing in a tournament in the poker room there.

And then we had enjoyed a wonderful half hour before sleeping.

That memory made me smile.

I strained to hear anything, at that point not thinking I was between moments in time. That usually takes me some focus to do and focus while I am sleeping is not one of my superpowers.

No sound.

My warning sense that something was very wrong was dinging in the back of my head like an annoying microwave timer that wouldn't shut off.

I rolled out of the big bed, shoving the thick tan comforter aside, and padded to the window across the soft brown carpet in my boxer shorts.

I pulled the blinds aside slightly and the night shade and after my eyes adjusted to the bright light, I knew instantly what the problem was.

There over Las Vegas, at about two thousand feet, was an airliner turning to make a final approach into the airport. Only it wasn't moving. It was just stuck there, as if someone had glued a decal to a phony blue-sky ceiling in a bedroom.

Now, don't get me wrong. I love my ability to step into a moment of time, out of the normal time flow. It's my second favorite superpower right behind being able to teleport. But unless I do the stepping between moments purposefully, or have another superhero or god put me in a time bubble, I didn't much like being out of whack with the real ticking of time.

I took a deep breath and imagined myself back in the normal flow of time. That's what I always did to drop a time bubble that I made.

Nothing.

Intense silence.

Not even the deep breath helped.

No wonder my alarm dinger was going off in the back of my head. Something was very wrong.

I headed for the bathroom. Patty Ledgerwood, aka Front Desk girl and my girlfriend, was in the shower, her head thrown back as water ran down her long brown hair.

Only the water wasn't actually running, more like glistening in sparkling droplets all over her as if someone had taken a still picture of her.

I can say without any chance of argument that she had a perfect body. And every detail, from her smooth skin to her deep brown eyes fit together.

Now I was no different than any other young man growing up. What stood frozen in front of me was any teenage boy's fantasy. A beautiful woman with a perfect body, naked in a shower, caught in a moment of sheer beauty, every perfect detail magnified by the wetness.

Even as a superhero, I wasn't immune to that, so for an instant after I opened the shower door, I stopped and stared.

Sometimes even emergencies can take a back seat to an opportunity of a lifetime.

So I stood there for a moment, just a moment, staring. Honest, it was only a moment.

And all I could do was ask myself how I had gotten so lucky as to have that woman in my life?

Finally I eased forward, feeling almost guilty, and touched her shoulder, bringing her into the time bubble with me.

The water around her ran off, but no more water came out of the faucet.

"Up for a rematch from last night?" she asked, turning to face me and giving me that smile that often made me forget everything around me.

And her being nude and wet like that was just damn near impossible for me to resist.

"In a little bit," I said, leaning forward and kissing her. "We have a problem I can't seem to get a handle on."

Her expression turned serious, and she turned to shut off the water. Then she realized it was no longer running, even though the faucet was turned on.

"Are we between moments in time?" she asked, looking at me.

Wow, another reason I loved this woman so much. She was scary smart. I nodded.

"How come?" she asked, quickly stepping past me and wrapping a blue bath towel around that fantastic body, making me slightly sad I had said anything.

"I woke up out of time," I said.

Back before I was a superhero, those were words I never would have imagined saying unless I was late for an appointment, or the start of a poker tournament.

"Can you clear us?"

I shook my head. "I don't think I did this one."

"Let's get some clothes on and call Stan," she said. "See if he has any idea what's happened."

"That's why I came to get you out of the shower," I said.

She laughed as she worked to dry off. "Sure it wasn't just to stare?"

"Well," I said as I headed back into the bedroom, "I did a little of that as well."

"Pervert," she shouted after me.

"Guilty and loving it," I shouted back.

I could hear her laugh as I worked to get dressed.

Chapter Two

Patty put on her comfortable clothes, which were jeans and a white blouse. She pulled her hair back and didn't bother with any make-up. She looked fantastic and I told her so.

I also had on jeans, but wore a tee-shirt under my black leather jacket and fedora-like hat that served as my Poker Boy uniform. The hat and coat somehow helped me focus energy. I didn't need them inside the apartment, but in emergency situations like this, I felt better having them on.

When we were both completely dressed and had breakfast bars half eaten, we moved into the center of Patty's living room. I had tried a couple of times to drop back into the normal flow, without success.

And I had Patty stand across the room from me and I made myself concentrate on releasing her.

Nothing.

Around us the tan furniture and tan rug seemed completely normal. Everything seemed normal except the clock on the wall near the kitchen door was stopped.

So I was stuck between instants of time, and from what I could tell, I had brought Patty into the mess as well. But if I hadn't, she would have been really, really mad at me. I just never considered not including her these days in anything I did. We were so much stronger together than we were on our own.

"Stan, a little help?" I said at the ceiling. For some reason, every time I called out to my boss, the God of Poker, I shouted upwards. I was fairly certain he could hear me if I just said his name softly, but the old habit died hard.

Patty and I both stood there in her living room, waiting. Usually he appeared almost instantly, but after about five seconds I looked at Patty and shook my head.

"Laverne?" I shouted at the ceiling, hoping that Lady Luck herself would hear me.

Nothing.

We had no access to my team this time around.

"Let me see if I can jump us to my office and get out of this," I said.

Instantly I had alarm bells go off in the back of my head and Patty touched my arm and shook her head. "That feels wrong."

"I agree," I said, pushing back the alarm bells.

My little voice was telling me the problem was here and we needed to stay here and solve this. But it was really, really odd that my calling Stan or Laverne couldn't get out of this. They never had had troubles with coming into time bubbles before.

I went over to the window in the living room and looked at the frozen city below. The cars on The Strip were frozen in place, a couple of birds were stopped in midair a few floors below, and flags on the top of a building across the street hung at odd angles, clearly blown by a wind, but yet not moving.

I looked back at Patty who stood there staring at me.

"Do you have any idea how many gods or superheroes have the power to take a person between moments of time?" I asked, moving back over toward her.

She shook her head slowly as she thought, her long brown hair flopping around on her back as she did. "It's not many, I know that. And you are the only superhero that I know that has that power."

I wasn't sure what to think of that, but at the moment I didn't let myself dwell on it.

"Seems we have some spare time on our hands," I said, smiling at the worried look on her face and in her wonderful dark-brown eyes. "We might as well enjoy it."

The worried look turned to puzzlement.

I shrugged.

"We're trapped in a moment in time," I said. "Someone did this. It's either a wide-spread thing or a focused event and

I'm betting on focused around the person who did it, since it takes some real power to hold a time bubble for very long that's very large. And to include us, it has to be pretty large, so I don't expect this to last that long."

She nodded. "Good point. Any way to know how far this bubble extends?"

I stopped and thought about that for a moment. In the past, when I held a time bubble, as I called them, keeping myself and others out of the flow of regular time, there was a limit. I once had a dog inside a time bubble and it couldn't get out, the edge of the bubble held it until I released the bubble.

I remember thinking that it would be a good and easy trap for anything wild, except that so far I hadn't learned how to project a bubble I wasn't inside of. And being trapped inside a time bubble with something wild hadn't really appealed to me, so I had tossed that idea out.

"I have a question," I said. "Was I supposed to be part of this bubble or just an accident?"

"If you are included only by accident, by bringing me in as well must be draining more energy," Patty said.

"Of whoever is doing this," I said.

"Let's go exploring and see if we can find the edge," I said, heading for the front door to her apartment.

Patty's apartment was on the seventeenth floor. Outside the corridor looked like a plush hotel hallway, with lamps scattered along the hallway and each door recessed into its own entryway.

The carpet was light blue and the walls painted off-white

with hotel-like art that depicted nothing hung on the walls. Four elevators were near the center of the building.

No one was in the hall.

"What's going to happen when we find the edge of the bubble?" Patty asked.

"My gut sense is that it will be like walking into a wall," I said. "So walk slow and protect your face."

"Good to know," she said, laughing and shaking her head.

We slowly walked the entire length of the hallway with arms extended in front of us. We must have looked pretty silly, almost walking like movie zombies.

No edge to be found.

"That's an impressive-sized bubble," I said when we reached the other end of the hallway and stopped.

There were two floors above hers and we headed for the stairs to the left and slowly worked our way upward.

We made it all the way to the top floor without finding the edge to the time bubble.

"This is someone very powerful," I said to Patty as we stood outside the stairway door in the upper hallway, the blue carpet making me feel more like standing on water than a floor. Here there were only four doors to the four expensive penthouses that filled this floor. I had no idea who lived on this floor, but my gut sense it was someone powerful and very rich in the local area.

The fear I was starting to feel suddenly twisted my stomach around the breakfast bar. I pushed it down and took a slow breath, getting my nerves under control.

"This might be generated mechanically," Patty said.

I looked around at the building and walls and windows and the lights on the walls. Damn she was smart and had the ability to see things I just flat missed.

"I think you might be right," I said. "This kind of field could be generated or amplified through the electrical system. So it would cover the entire building like a skin. A mechanical field might block calling out to Stan or Laverne because natural fields have never blocked me calling them before."

"Good thing we didn't try jumping out of here," she said.

"We'd have smashed right into the bubble wall," I said, glad our warning senses had stopped us. "That might have been painful or worse."

She nodded. "We still don't know why anyone would do this."

"I'm getting the sense that whoever did this is not after us," I said. "My warning bells are not going off, except when I suggested we jump to the office."

"Neither are mine," Patty said. "I bet that whoever did this didn't realize you were here and that the time field wouldn't get to you."

"I wonder why it didn't," I said.

"We'll ask Stan about that later," Patty said, smiling at what must have been my puzzled look. "Now we need to figure out who is doing this and why."

However, I had no idea how to find out that simple thing.

At that moment, the stairwell door at the other end of the hall rattled and stated to open.

"Freeze," I whispered to Patty and we both struck a pose we could hold that made us look like we were just two people frozen in time standing in the hallway.

It looked like we were going to find out who was doing this sooner, rather than later.

CHAPTER THREE

"There you are," Stan, the God of Poker, said as he came through the stairwell door and into the hall.

I released the breath I think I had been holding and relaxed.

Stan had on his normal button-down sweater and tan slacks. He could blend in anywhere and right now he seemed to almost blend in with the hallway as well, even though his colors seemed to clash with the blue carpet. It wouldn't surprise me if I looked away and looked back, he would be wearing blue slacks.

Right behind him was Screamer, dressed in jeans and a dress shirt with the sleeves rolled up. Screamer was a superhero who worked for the police. He got his name because he could put images in criminal's minds that made them scream in terror.

He was my height at about six foot and had intense dark eyes that seemed to see through things.

Through the door behind Screamer came Ben, a god in the library area and the oldest of our team. He was panting from climbing the stairs.

I had no idea how old Ben really was, but his old-fashioned suits and wrinkled face and hands made him look like a grandfather from a classic movie.

I was very, very glad to see them.

"Did you hear my call?" I asked as Patty and I stepped toward them.

"I did," Stan said. "But I couldn't jump into the building, so I stopped time for me and Ben and Screamer and we managed to merge fields with this time field down in the lobby."

"Twenty floors. Long climb," Ben said, still panting.

"So ever seen anything like this before?" I asked Stan. "Ever have anyone do a time bubble this large?"

He shook his head. "And neither has Laverne. It basically covers this entire building like a skin."

"More than likely run through the electrical system," I said.

Stan looked at me for a moment, clearly thinking, then nodded. "Possible."

"But why?" Patty said.

"I've been wondering the same thing," Screamer said.

"As have I," Ben said, still panting slightly.

"Anyone in a personal time bubble," Patty said, "can walk around just fine without generating something this large to take an entire building out of time. You would get the same effect with just a personal bubble."

That very problem had been bothering me as well. Clearly, if Stan and the rest entered down on the main floor and came up, the bubble holding this building was in the walls and covered the entire building. Patty was right, there was no reason to do that.

None.

Unless...

"Maybe doing something like this," I said, sort of sweeping my arms around me in a grand fashion, "in the walls or electrical wiring of a building, is the only way for whoever did this to generate a time bubble field."

"Mechanical only," Ben said, nodding. "Not a god power. Possible."

"Seen anything like this before?" Patty asked just a fraction of a second before I could.

"Crystals," Ben said, nodding. "In the old Atlantis days."

It always freaked me out a little when someone I knew as a regular person here in Las Vegas started talking about Atlantis. Not the casino, the actual continent and civilization that had actually existed and then had been destroyed. And more often than not, that person had actually been alive during the time of Atlantis.

Stan nodded. "I sort of remember hearing something like that from Laverne once."

"Do you remember who was doing it back then?" I asked Ben, then realized how stupid my question was. His memory was amazing and he could remember every detail and information in every book he had ever read.

"The God of Electricity," Ben said. "Actually, the real experiments in time and electrical powers were done by her assistant."

"Oh, no," Stan said, shaking his head.

Screamer and Patty and I just stared at my boss until Screamer finally said, "You want to fill us in on the problem?"

Ben nodded and took over from Stan, who for the God of Poker, looked suddenly very upset.

"Far before Atlantis, a giant by the name of Arges was the God of Lightning. He was a fan of Zeus and gave him the power to fire electrical bolts, which is why Zeus became known after centuries as being able to use lightning as a weapon."

I so wanted to ask about so much of this, because as I had discovered in my short years of being a superhero, the gods of mythology had often existed, and some of them still did. I had never heard if Zeus was still around, and had never had the courage to ask, to be honest.

Ben went on, with me saying nothing.

"When the gods and the giants managed to banish the Titans to the city that lies under Las Vegas, Arges was injured in the battle and he stepped down and gave his duties over to his daughter, who was a god. He died from his injuries before Atlantis came into being."

"Who was his daughter?" I asked.

Ben looked at me very puzzled, then said, "I need to spend some time with you getting you up to speed on the history of the gods, don't I?"

"I've been saying that," I said. "At least to myself."

"When this is over," Ben said, giving me that grandfather look he sometimes gave me, "we'll make the time."

"Laverne is Arges's daughter," Stan said. "Back in Atlantis, as Laverne was taking over more and more duties, she gave the duty of electricity to the Goddess Horae, a good friend of hers who also had control over planting and seasons and things like that."

"And a young man, a superhero of sorts," Ben said, "began work for Horae as Atlantis boomed. Over the centuries there, he got himself in and out of many troubles with his experiments with electricity and using it in different forms of travel and controlling time."

"What's his name?" Patty asked, again right before I could.

Ben shrugged. "Nothing worth pronouncing right now. Last I heard, in Atlantis, he went by Nicky."

"Still a superhero?" Screamer asked.

Ben nodded. "Last time I heard, still officially working for Horae, when or if she can ever track him down. He used to throw some wild parties, which is what caused part of his problems."

"And he could do things like this time bubble over the building?" I asked Ben.

"More than likely he could."

I didn't like the sounds of that. "When was the last time anyone saw him?"

Ben glanced at Stan, who only shrugged. "Atlantis," Ben said, "about sixty years before it was destroyed."

Okay, that silenced our little group standing in the blue and white plush hallway inside a giant time bubble.

For some reason my friends thought a guy who hadn't been seen in more thousands of years than I wanted to think about had done this to a modern apartment building here in Las Vegas.

I managed to not laugh. "I think we need another suspect."

And that also sent the entire group back into silence.

CHAPTER FOUR

"There are no other suspects," Screamer said after a moment of silence in the hallway.

I just didn't think a guy who hadn't been seen since Atlantis was the logical choice, so I changed the point of focus.

"How about we do a search of the entire building," I said. "See if we can find anyone moving."

Stan and Ben both nodded, so I sent Ben and Screamer to one apartment, Stan to another, and Patty and I would handle a third on this floor. Then we would check the last one and work our way down.

However, the search ended just about as quickly as it started.

As we neared the four doors to the four penthouses near the elevators, modern jazz dance music blared out over the hallway, almost vibrating one of the doors. The music seemed to be right out of the 1940s big band era.

Patty looked at me with a puzzled look and all I could do was shrug.

"That form of music was very popular in Atlantis," Ben said softly.

I just shook my head for a moment. Great, just great. Maybe this Nicky guy was inside.

I had no idea what I was walking into, but with Stan at my side and Patty and Ben and Screamer close behind, I used one of my superpowers to unlock the door and slowly eased it open, letting the intense loud music smack me in the face. It sounded like an entire band was just around the corner in the main area of the penthouse apartment.

And then, over the intense music, I caught the sound of laughing and talking.

Lots of laughing and lots of talking. Actually more like shouting, since that was all anyone could do over that amount of noise.

I eased around a corner of the entryway so I could see the huge main room of the penthouse and then just stood there, my mouth open, staring at about fifty people dancing, all dressed in brightly-colored robes and togas and all barefoot on the plush white carpet. The expensive white furniture had been pushed back to the sides to form the large dance floor.

The main room of the big apartment was completely full of people.

Everyone was young and all clearly having a great time.

I felt like I had walked into a college frat party. I hated drunken kids' parties when in college, thought them stupid beyond words and never went to a one, mostly because I never joined a fraternity or any other group for that matter.

I didn't much care for the party I was staring at either.

There were so many colors jumping up and down and swirling around, I almost got dizzy trying to watch it.

Suddenly, one of the dancers on the edge of the mob spotted us and smiled and broke away from his partner, a blonde with far too much long hair that seemed to function as a second robe and only allowed glimpses of her smiling face.

The guy coming toward us had long brown hair that looked like it was cut by putting a bowl over his head. He had on a brown robe that seemed a cross between a bathrobe and a toga.

He was smiling a huge smile that lit up his face and the smile reached his eyes. Beads of sweat had formed on his forehead from the dancing and I noticed the apartment had started to heat up.

None of my alarms were going off about him, so he wasn't a threat. At least I didn't think my alarms had sounded. Even inside my own head, I wasn't certain I would have heard them in this noise.

The music still pounded at me like a hammer and I could tell it was everything Patty could do to not cover her ears.

As the kid got closer, he went straight at Ben and gave him a hug.

"Uncle Ben," the kid shouted over the noise. "What are you doing here?"

Finally Stan couldn't take it any longer. He took us out of time, instantly silencing the music. I almost staggered at the relief.

"Thank you," Patty sighed softly.

Screamer just shook his head as if trying to clear it.

I didn't know it was possible to have a time bubble inside another time bubble, but it seemed it was. Thankfully.

My ears were ringing and even with that I could tell this guy wasn't a threat.

All the dancers were now frozen in wild positions of movements, bright-colored robes and hair flung all over the place. From a few of the loose robes, I could tell that underwear wasn't a fashion these kids believed in.

"Sorry," the kid who had hugged Ben said, still smiling. "A little loud I suppose, but figured we weren't bothering anyone."

Ben just shook his head and turned to face Stan and the rest of us. "This is my nephew, Nicky."

"From Atlantis?" I blurted out, not even wanting to know how he was Ben's nephew.

"Where else?" Nicky asked, still smiling.

Oh, wow. And I thought I had a lot to learn about history.

Chapter Five

en introduced us all.

Nicky gave Patty a very broad smile and a slight kiss on the back of her hand. He was a real charmer, this guy.

After the introductions, Ben said, "Your mother and Horae have both been very worried about you."

I didn't want to even ask who his mother was.

Nicky actually looked puzzled at that and my alarm bells suddenly went off at full force. This kid had no idea where or when he was.

Not a clue.

"Nicky," I said, indicating the kid should come with me, "I want to show you something."

Ben nodded and I led the young superhero across the

room toward the big windows. The others followed me through the frozen crowd until we all stood beside one of the huge floor-to-ceiling windows.

I pointed at The Strip below and then at the desert around the city. "You know where you are?"

He shrugged, looking out over the city. "Never seen the place before," he said. "North quadrant, maybe."

"North quadrant of what?" I asked as Ben shook his head and looked down at the soft white carpet.

"Of Atlantis," Nicky said. "Where else."

I turned to Ben. "What was this area called in the time of Atlantis?"

"This was mostly all ocean and swamp," Ben said softly. "This land mass was much lower at the time, so we really had no name for this area."

Nicky looked at me, then at his uncle, a look of panic starting to cross his face.

"What exactly did you do to make this building be in a time bubble?" I asked.

"Any building," Nicky said. "We all jam into a mountain cabin that I put the bubble around. I can jump the field out of time and have it go around a larger building. That gives us all a place to party and not even be gone more than an hour or so."

"How do you pick the building?" I asked.

He shrugged, looking out over the city below. "I don't. My machine does. Chronos is going to be angry at me for jumping in time, isn't he?"

I ignored that question. "How do all these people get here?"

"Portal near the device down on the ground floor," Nicky said. "Everyone was already in the cabin before I locked up the building. So a portal down on the main floor is the only way in and out. When exactly is this?"

Silence. I couldn't answer him because I honestly didn't know the answer.

Finally Ben said softly, "This time is about eleven thousand years after Atlantis was destroyed."

"Destroyed?" Nicky asked, looking like he might faint at any moment.

"You haven't been seen since about sixty years ahead of the destruction, Ben said."

Now the kid simply dropped to the floor, his eyes blank, his smile long gone.

So we had a young inventor superhero that had brought about fifty people with him through time to the present. We couldn't let him or any of them just go back, because in this history, our history, my history, he didn't go back.

This was going to take a time travel expert far, far smarter than I was to unravel the mess that Nicky had just caused.

I looked around at all the dancers frozen in a moment of pure enjoyment, then down at the young man sitting on the floor staring down at the depths of the plush carpet.

My warning voice was tingling.

Something was still very, very wrong. And I needed to figure out what.

But for the life of me, at the moment I just couldn't ask poor Nicky another question.

Not after the reality he just faced.

CHAPTER SIX

We all stood there in silence until finally what had been worrying me crawled its ugly way to the surface of my mind. And when it poked out, I shuddered.

I turned to my team, letting Nicky sit on the floor and stew in his own thoughts.

"If this time bubble gets shut off, the bubble is going to haul us back to the past as well with it."

"But it doesn't go back to the past," Stan said, staring at the dancers. "We know that because Nicky disappears."

"In this timeline," I said.

Stan started to open his mouth and shut it, suddenly lost in his thoughts.

"Have I ever said that time travel gives me a headache?" I asked.

Patty smiled at me as I turned and kneeled down beside Nicky.

"How is this time bubble around the building set to recall?"

"One day exactly from the moment it left," he said. "Automatically. It will return within thirty minutes of leaving."

"And it takes everyone who is inside it at that moment with it?"

"I don't know," he said, shrugging. "I would assume so. This is the first time I've ever tried it. I figured if the bubble took along anyone who didn't belong, I would just send the hitchhikers back where they belonged before they noticed."

Now my stomach was really twisting. We had an untested machine that could take us all at any moment.

I stood and looked at Patty. "Any idea how many people live in this building?"

"Oh, my," she said, her face white. "Maybe around 500 people at any given time."

It was the middle of the afternoon on a Saturday, so not all of them would be in the building, but a large number of them would be.

Stan and Ben and Screamer had been listening and all three of them were just shaking their heads slowly, Stan staring at the dancers.

All my team looked like I was feeling.

Shocked.

Around us, all of Nicky's friends from Atlantis remained

frozen in different positions of dance, their brightly-colored robes spread out or twisted around them, smiles covering their faces.

If we were inside this building when it shifted back, we would end up in a timeline where Nicky returned to Atlantis with his friends. And everyone from Las Vegas time in this building would go with him and suddenly find themselves thousands of years in the past. And all of them would be lost to this world and all their families.

That would be a missing person's case for the ages.

And if we stopped this, Nicky and his friends would be stuck here, lost to all their families.

And since it was a new invention, who knew if the timer was right or would even work.

Or if it went off, where or when it would send any of us.

Wonderful. Just wonderful.

We were so screwed.

I had to admit, Nicky here had really invented something to cause problems.

"I'm open to ideas," I said, glancing around at my team.

I didn't even have one of my normally stupid ideas or random thoughts.

Patty, Screamer, Ben, and Stan all just stood there looking blankly. We all seemed to understand this was a disaster where no matter what we did, no one won.

"So what's going on?" Laverne demanded as she walked into the room. Lady Luck had on her normal power suit and her hair was pulled back. She also had on tennis shoes instead of her normal dress shoes. More than likely she knew she was going to have to climb twenty flights of stairs when she came into the time bubble.

She looked at the crowd of frozen dancers with a puzzled frown, then looked at Ben. "Why are those kids dressed like they are from an Atlantis college party?"

"Because they are," Ben said.

That made the frown on Lady Luck's face just get deeper.

Behind me, Nicky was climbing to his feet. "Hi, Aunt Laverne," he said, stepping up beside me, his voice soft and his eyes not meeting hers, but instead staying focused firmly on the carpet in front of him.

"Oh, shit," Lady Luck said, seeing him. She clearly understood the situation, or at least part of it, instantly.

She stepped forward and seemed to tower over the cowering Nicky.

"So you are responsible for the greatest mystery in all of Atlantis, the Lost Fifty," she said.

She glanced at Stan, then focused back on Nicky.

Ben was nodding slowly, his gaze also aimed directly at the carpet.

Nicky wisely said nothing.

Lady Luck shook her head, clearly disgusted and saying nothing. Having Lady Luck disgusted at me was my worst nightmare. And I had some horrid nightmares at times, but having her disgusted at me was the worst one.

Finally, Lady Luck turned to look at the frozen dancers, then at Stan, touching his arm slightly for a moment, and then finally she looked at me. "We can't let these kids go back. They did not return in this timeline. They were lost to their families a very long time ago."

I nodded.

"We know that," I said. "But we have another problem as well. Nicky thinks his machine will just take everyone in the building when it automatically jumps."

Beside me Nicky nodded.

"Even the people from this time period who are in time stasis in the building?" Laverne asked, her voice as cold and as angry as I could ever imagine it getting. The windows seemed to vibrate from the tension in her words.

I know I did.

"I think so," Nicky said. "I don't know for sure. It might. I don't know."

I thought the poor kid was going to break into tears, but somehow he just kept staring at the carpet and managed to hold it together.

"Can you just shut it off?" I asked Nicky. I hoped my voice was a little less angry and powerful as Laverne's, but I was so mad at this point, I wasn't sure.

Nicky did exactly as I feared he would do. He shook his head.

"It will return the moment I shut it off," he said.

"Perfect, just perfect," I said to myself. "Where is it exactly?"

"Ground floor, very center of the building," Nicky said.

"Does it have a visible timer on it?"

Again he shook his head.

"Any other way outside this field but through the door on the ground floor?" Stan asked.

Again Nicky just shook his head.

I was stunned. Not only had this kid just destroyed the lives of fifty of his closest friends and their families, if we didn't figure something out quickly, he was going to take all of us as well and who knew how many hundreds with him in this building.

"How long do we have before the time field returns to Atlantis?" Laverne asked directly at Nicky.

"At most ten hours," he said. Then softly he said, "It might be a lot less. I'm sorry."

"Not as sorry as you're going to be when your mother hears about this," Laverne said.

Then Lady Luck turned to me and said simply.

"I'll talk with Chronos and the Fates and see if I can come up with a solution. In the meantime, get everyone out of this building. I'll have the portal downstairs hooked into real time to move with your time here in the building."

I had no idea how she was going to do that, but decided this was not the time to ask.

Then with Nicky by the arm, she turned and yanked the poor kid by the arm toward the apartment door like a mother with a misbehaving three-year-old.

CHAPTER SEVEN

e all watched them go. I looked at the fifty dancers and took a deep breath. "We're going to need help and a really amazing cover story for the residents."

"And we're going to need counselors for these kids." Patty said, indicating the dancers, "to help them understand what happened."

"They aren't even going to be speaking English," Ben said. "Nicky could because he's a superhero, but none of these kids will."

"Can we give it to them in some sort of power?" I asked, trying to imagine fifty college kids trying to learn English while dealing with being centuries out of time and their entire country being destroyed and their families killed.

Ben nodded slowly. "We might. For the Atlantis Fifty, we might be able to make exceptions. I'll go find out.

"See if you can find something that will ease their memories as well," I said.

Ben looked at the group of frozen dancers and nodded sadly, understanding exactly what I was saying. With that, he turned and headed for the door and the stairwell for the long climb down.

I turned to Screamer. "We're going to need Johnny's help on this and any other police we can trust. And a bunch more we're going to have to fool with a cover story."

Johnny was Detective Johnny State. He was also a super-hero working for the police department. I had worked with Johnny on numbers of cases, including the first case when I met Patty.

"That's going to take a really good cover story," Screamer said.

"Some sort of phony virus," I said, "that everyone in the building might have been exposed to, so we take everyone to a holding area and then when the time bubble jumps, we let them return, giving them all clear."

I was making this up as I went, but that sounded like it might work. We get the Atlantis Fifty, as Ben called the dancers frozen around us, out first and isolated, then we work on the normal residents.

"I'll get some help from the gods of health," Patty said, "to come up with something logical, but not too bad, but that would require this kind of action."

"Stan," I said, turning to my boss. "If you can hold this time bubble inside Nicky's bubble, do you think it's going to be possible to release a set area of residents from his mechanical bubble?"

Stan shook his head, turning his attention from the dancers. "I don't think so. It doesn't work that way, and since this is mechanical, I doubt I can block it."

"How did I release Patty?" I asked.

"She's a superhero," Stan said.

I thought I was discouraged before, now I was really about to lose it.

"Oh, no," Patty said, shaking her head.

I took a deep breath and came up with the only solution I could think of.

"So we move maybe up to five hundred frozen people by stretcher to the entrance, down flights of stairs. Nothing to it, right?"

Silence in a room full of dancers.

I turned to the love of my life. "We're going to need even more help from the medical side of this than we thought," I said. "Because everyone has to be taken by ambulance to the hospital. Only way any cover story will work when they all snap back into real time going out that doorway Laverne is setting up."

Patty nodded.

"Our cover story could be some gas that knocked them all out," I said. "And has no lasting problems with it."

"Better than a virus," Screamer said, nodding.

I turned to Screamer. "Johnny's going to need his girl-friend from the paper to cover this as well. We're going to need help to keep this from turning into a panic that will empty the city."

Again everyone stood silently.

Then Patty said simply, "I don't think we have enough time."

"Time is the enemy no matter what we do," I said.

"Ain't that the truth," Screamer said.

I kissed Patty and told her to get going.

She nodded and went with Screamer out the door almost at a run.

I looked at my boss. "Can you hold the dancers?" I asked.

He nodded.

"I'm going to go scout out where the local residents are to save a little time while we're waiting for the cavalry to arrive."

He nodded and dropped down onto a couch, staring at the Atlantis Fifty, saying nothing.

There just wasn't any more to say at the moment. All I knew was that I didn't really want to see Atlantis. At least not on a one-way ticket to a time sixty years before it was destroyed.

CHAPTER EIGHT

I checked out the other penthouse apartments. They were really nice, and luckily no one was home in any of them.

On the floor below there were six apartments, all the size of Patty's apartment.

In two I found guys watching television. In two others I found only a woman home, both of them also watching television. The other two apartments were empty.

I was starting to understand how really lucky we had gotten that this happened on a Saturday afternoon.

On the floor above Patty's, I found twelve people in the six apartments. Four were playing cards in one, two kids about twenty-something were making love and were pretty tangled up together, which was going to get interesting to say the least.

They both might need counseling after this was over, one moment going at it with their partner, the next on a stretcher going out the front door of the building.

So in three floors I had sixteen people.

I heard some commotion in the staircase outside and went out to find Patty and Screamer headed back up.

I went with them back to the top floor and back into the room full of the brightly clothed dancers.

Stan was still just sitting there, seemingly lost in his own thoughts.

"Medical equipment and ambulances are headed this way," Patty said. "We've got all the gods and superheroes who could get free working this. But not everyone outside is with us, so we'll have to be careful outside the building."

"Are they coming up with stretchers?" I asked and Patty nodded. 'They should arrive here in about ten minutes."

"No one I could find on this floor," I said. "But we'll need to check again to make sure."

"Police already have the building surrounded and roads blocked off and press held back," Screamer said. "Johnny and two people he can trust are coming up in a few minutes."

Less than thirty minutes. I was impressed.

"So now we have to get these kids moving," Stan said.

"I think we should wait for Ben and Laverne," I said. "We have a language problem."

"I speak their language," Stan said softly.

I kind of looked at my boss, who seemed very, very upset

by all this. Usually he was calm and clear, but now he just sat staring at the dancers.

I glanced at Patty and she shrugged.

"You want to tell me what's going on," I said to my boss, going over and dropping onto the couch beside him.

"We don't have time," he said, shaking his head, but not moving to stand.

"I want to wait for Laverne and Ben and help from other gods to help ease these kids' transition," I said firmly. "They can all walk down anyhow. So taking the time is worth the gamble."

He nodded, clearly agreeing.

"So what happened?"

My little voice sort of told me the answer, so I went ahead and asked anyway. "Did you know some of these kids?"

He nodded.

"Which ones?" I asked, my voice gentle. It never would have occurred to me that I would have to be gentle with my boss, the God of Poker.

"The two twins," he said, pointing to two brown-haired girls dancing almost back-to-back near the center.

Patty gasped and I sort of did the same the moment I focused on them. They looked just like Stan.

"Are they superheroes?" I asked softly.

"Not yet," he said. "They will be."

"Your daughters?"

He nodded.

All I wanted to do was be sick.

Chapter Nine

All four of us remained silent after that until Ben and Laverne suddenly appeared on the edge of the room.

"Thank you," Ben said to her.

"We can teleport inside the bubble?" I asked.

Laverne nodded.

I turned to Patty.

She was ahead of me, already turning for the door. "I'll cancel the stretchers coming up, have them stage on the main floor. I'll get it set up."

Being able to teleport inside this bubble was the first good news we had gotten in this mess.

I stood and Laverne looked at Stan, a feeling of complete sadness on her face.

"Stan, you should be able to bring your daughters out before we do the rest," she said. "Get them out of here."

He nodded, took a deep breath and stood. "I'll explain what happened and they will help get their friends rescued. Give us a few minutes."

Laverne started to object, then nodded.

Then Stan moved into the dancers and touched one daughter on the shoulder, than the other, bringing them out of the time bubble he had the rest of the dancers in.

"Dad," the one closest to the window said, glancing around at her frozen friends. "What are you doing?"

"Yeah, does mom know you are breaking up our party?" the other asked.

Stan shuddered and then with another deep breath said, "Follow me."

I glanced at Ben and he waved that I should not ask, even though at that moment I would have never asked.

In my head I heard Laverne's voice. *His first wife killed herself when they lost their two daughters. Never ask him about it, ever.*

Understood, I thought back at her.

Stan took his two daughters toward a bedroom in the back of the huge penthouse. I did not envy him at all what he was about to tell those two girls.

I couldn't even comprehend it, to be honest. It just made my stomach twist into little knots.

Laverne looked at me, then nodded that I should go ahead with the plan.

"Let's give Stan the time," I said. "I will start clearing out residents, jumping them to the main floor. There should be a place down there we can store them until stretchers can take them outside."

Laverne nodded, staring at the door where Stan and his daughters had vanished.

"Ben, you stay here to help when Stan and his daughters need the help."

He nodded.

"Screamer," I said. "I know where people are on the two floors below. Go down to Patty's floor and start scouting. And work with Johnny when he gets here."

"Got it," Screamer said and turned and headed for the door.

"Stop a moment," Lady Luck said to Screamer. She waved a hand at him. "I just unblocked what was holding you from learning how to teleport."

She turned to me. "Have him jump with you on the first couple, then he can start moving people down as well. Have Johnny and his people do the scouting ahead."

Screamer started to open his mouth, his eyes wide, then he said simply, "Thank you."

Lady Luck waved her hand and sat down on the couch were Stan had been sitting. "You earned it and you would have figured it out eventually, and now you and my daughter can be together easier."

I smiled and grabbed his arm before he could say anything. He was married to Sherri, one of Lady Luck's daughters, and she lived in Reno while he lived here in Vegas.

I jumped us one floor down to where a guy was sitting in shorts and a tee-shirt watching a football game. The apartment was done in brown tones and had heavy tan drapes blocking out the sun. The television he was watching was huge and from what I could tell, the program was in commercial.

The guy looked to be around sixty and slightly overweight.

"Holy crap, what just happened?" Screamer asked, looking at me.

"Lady Luck just helped you get another power. Don't question it. You'll have time to figure it all out later. We got a lot of people and our own butts to save."

Screamer nodded.

I walked across the room. "See this spot?" I asked, pointing at the carpet beside me.

He nodded.

"Jump to it."

"How?" he asked, looking puzzled.

"I imagine myself in the new spot and then think I am there."

He nodded, focused at the spot beside me, and the next instant he was there, facing past me at the drawn drapes of the apartment.

"It worked," he said softly, shaking his head. "I thought the word *jump* and it happened."

"That sometimes works for me as well," I said. "Jump into the kitchen next." I pointed at the open kitchen on the other side of a brown counter with barstools against it.

Almost instantly he was there.

Then he jumped back beside me.

"Wow, just wow," he said. He was smiling like a kid at Christmas getting everything he asked for.

"I'm going to jump this guy and both of us to the main floor area," I said. "You can work on more there."

He nodded and I imagined the frozen guy and Screamer linked to me and I jumped to the main floor of the apartment building.

I was surprised to see so much activity going on. It was lucky I had tucked us off into a corner, otherwise someone might have seen us appear.

Patty sensed me at once and came running over.

The guy I had jumped with was on the floor, his back against the wall.

"Screamer can now teleport," I told her. "Where do we bring the residents down to so we aren't seen?"

Patty nodded to Screamer and smiled. "Great, we're going to need the help."

Then she showed us an area near the freight elevator where two people were setting up thick mats to help the residents of the building not get hurt. It was tucked around a corner and was big enough to get stretchers in close, but yet not be seen by anyone who shouldn't see people appearing and disappearing.

"We're telling people we're bringing people down the freight elevator and staircase here," she said. "We already have everyone who was on this level out and on the way to the hospital in ambulances."

I kissed her quickly. "Great job. We'll be back with more shortly."

She nodded and I turned to Screamer. "Remember the spot in that last apartment?"

He nodded.

"Jump there."

He vanished.

I followed him and he was standing there in the apartment smiling when I arrived.

"So how do I jump when I don't know where I'm going?" he asked.

"You know," I said.

He frowned.

"The apartment next door has a man in it," I said. "Can you sort of sense it, sense the apartment?"

After a moment he nodded slowly.

"Jump there, get the guy and I'll meet you downstairs."

"Do I have to touch the guy to jump him?" Screamer asked.

"Just imagine a link between you and the person. And then when you get ready to jump, imagine that link solid and that person coming with you."

"Wow, our minds are powerful, aren't they?"

"Don't question it," I said, smiling at him. "Like walking. Never think about it. Just do it."

He nodded and then vanished.

I went to get the woman from the apartment across the hall.

Screamer beat me to the main floor with his person, but not by much.

Chapter Ten

Johnny and two other superheroes working for the Las Vegas Police scouted apartments ahead of Screamer and me as we worked our way down the building floor-by-floor.

It seemed to be taking much, much longer than it needed to take, but we were making sure that no one was missed.

At one point Patty told me between jumps that Stan and Laverne and Ben had jumped all the kids to the main floor and had them all walk out into two waiting Greyhound buses. She said that they got safely away from the building and were being taken to a large lodge in the mountains where they could get the kids help and let them rest and get them started on learning what they were going to need to learn to survive in this new world.

"And counseling, I hope," I said.

"I can't imagine why not," Patty said, a very sad look on her face. "They all lost everything today. Their parents, their families, their entire world. Everything they knew and took for granted is gone."

I just shook my head. I didn't want to let myself think about the Atlantis Fifty at the moment. Screamer and I needed to keep going.

So I kissed her and thanked her for telling me and jumped to the next person.

Two other gods from hotel and apartment management areas joined in helping Screamer and me when we reached the eleventh floor since they could teleport. Four of us were about as fast as the ambulances could handle the load of people. Luckily the hospital was very close.

And since none of the residents of the building were actually sick, they all would be released fairly quickly.

As the hours went by, Patty made sure the main floor was cleared of anyone who didn't need to be in the building.

Screamer and I were bringing down the last two residents from the third floor. Both were young women who had been having coffee together at an apartment kitchen counter.

The second floor had already been emptied by the two gods from Patty's area. They were now all gone.

Patty and two others were waiting with stretchers. Both of the others looked like paramedics. Both paramedics were young women and intent in their job.

They helped the two residents we had brought down carefully on to the stretchers and covered them.

"This is it," I said. "Let's all get out of here."

We turned for the door.

We didn't make it.

So close.

Chapter Eleven

A shimmering went through the air.

It seemed the lights blinked, but I couldn't be sure on that.

The world spun for just a second, then snapped down solid again.

I glanced around.

Patty, Screamer, two superhero paramedics from the medical world, and the two building residents were standing around me in a cabin that smelled of pine and a cold fireplace. Everyone had a shocked and worried look.

I was sure I was no exception to that.

Only a couple lights were on in the big, high-ceilinged room and curtains were pulled tight over the big windows.

"Oh, no," Patty said softly.

"We didn't make it," Screamer said.

One of the residents of the building looked around and asked, "What just happened?"

Screamer nodded to the superhero paramedics and then reached over and touched the two residents lightly. They both fell instantly asleep.

The paramedics caught them both and stretched the residents safely out onto the floor.

That would take care of that problem for a while at least.

I wanted to just sit on the floor with them and bang my fists, but instead I walked over to the closed main door of the big wooden cabin and eased it open. The hinges on the big wooden door actually had the decency to squeak.

The air outside smelled fresh and warm, like the day might be getting warmer soon. The wonderful scent of pine needles hit me next.

The cabin sat on a hillside covered in tall pine-like trees and in the distance I could see the blue hint of a lake.

Tucked off to one side of the cabin were ten cars like I had never seen. They all looked like they had been designed by a 1950s movie guy trying to imagine what a car of the future would look like.

One of them even had a bubble on it that covered six different seats.

They looked very, very much out of place in the rustic mountain setting.

Those cars were the transportation for the Atlantis Fifty, more than likely.

A highway seemed to wind along the hill below. From

where we were, I could hear high humming sounds that seemed to come from the vehicles buzzing past.

Not gas engines, that was for sure.

Patty stepped up beside me and looked around for a moment.

Then I pushed us both back into the cabin and shut the door.

"Are we where I think we are?" Screamer asked, standing next to the paramedics above the two residents stretched out on the floor.

"We're not in Kansas anymore, that's for sure," I said.

I took a deep breath and tried to think about jumping to my office hovering over Vegas.

Nothing. It wasn't there.

We were over eleven thousand years in the past. And who knew on what timeline.

In other words, we were screwed.

I looked around at the four others expecting me to lead them. I didn't have a clue what to do.

That silence just got too heavy.

"We stay here for a time," I said, finally, trying to sound decisive and in charge. Better than sitting on the floor pounding my fists.

But not much.

"You think Laverne might be able to get to us?" Screamer asked.

I shrugged. "Laverne or Chronos. We have no other hope otherwise, other than to get off this continent in the next sixty years and find a place to live and survive. So we sit tight for now and make it easier on them if they can rescue us."

All four of them nodded, clearly feeling as stunned as I felt. No one wanted to talk anymore about the fine mess we found ourselves in. I was okay with that.

"What happens when they come looking for the missing kids," Screamer asked.

I looked at him. "When that happens, we had better be gone. Somewhere."

That really nailed the silence so we all started looking around.

The place was bigger than it looked at first glance and that Nicky had described. It had a nice living room tucked over to one side with a large stone fireplace and a bunch of comfortable-looking couches and big chairs, all in dark brown tones that seemed to go well with the wood. The couches and chairs weren't shaped that different from anything you would see in a modern furniture store.

The ceiling was high and peaked and had wood beams.

On the opposite side was a kitchen and beyond that what looked like a bathroom. I had a hunch from the looks of those cars out front that using a bathroom in Atlantis might just be a learning experience.

Fifty people would have had no trouble being in here.

I turned to Screamer. "Help me find Nicky's machine."

He nodded and we started for a hallway that led off to what must be bedrooms of some sort.

"How long will they be out?" one of the paramedics asked, pointing at the two women on the floor.

"We haven't been introduced," I said, suddenly realizing I didn't know two of the people I was stuck with. I stopped and turned back. "I'm Poker Boy, this is Screamer, this is Patty."

The one paramedic with short blonde hair said, "My name is Katie."

"I'm Rocha," the taller one with short brown hair said.

Both were clearly in great shape and very strong from their handshakes.

We all did the pleasant stuff, as much as five people can do when trapped thousands of years from home in a world we didn't know. Then Screamer answered Katie's question.

"They will be out eight hours at least," Screamer said. "All harmless, I assure you."

The paramedic superhero nodded. "Let's get them back on a bed if there are any in this place."

"Hang on," I said, and went down the hallway and opened the first door on the right. It was a bedroom all right with a very comfortable large bed that seemed huge.

I jumped the two sleeping building residents onto the bed.

"Might want to straighten them out a little and cover them up," I said.

Katie nodded thanks at me and went into the bedroom.

"Can I do that?" Screamer asked.

I smiled at my friend. "I sure don't see why not."

"I'm going to check out the food supplies," Patty said.

"I'll help you," Rocha said, following her. "I'm hungry."

When she said that I realized I was as well, but I doubted I could eat at the moment.

Screamer and I quickly found Nicky's machine. It was in the bedroom on the left, sitting right in the middle of the floor.

Honestly, it looked more like someone had taken a motor out of a lawn mower and hooked it to the top of some plastic dome.

Only it was like no internal combustion engine I had ever seen. It had what looked like a big blue crystal sticking out of the top of it like a gearshift.

It wasn't humming or making any noise at all. In fact, it didn't even seem to have switches to turn it on or off. But it was glowing slightly.

"Any ideas?" I asked Screamer.

"Besides not touching it?" he said. "Not a one."

We headed back out and joined the other three in the kitchen area.

"Anyone here alive in Atlantis time?" I asked.

I had learned a long time ago that sometimes a superhero or a god could surprise you with how old they were. Since none of us aged much at all after we came into our powers, living a long time seemed to be an option. Ben looked moderately old, but he had been around for far longer than Atlantis. In fact, more than likely, he was here somewhere.

And we knew that Stan and Laverne were living here somewhere as well.

But I don't think we dared contact them. At least not until we gave Laverne some time to mount a rescue operation from our own time.

Of course, since it was time travel, the rescue might come in one hundred years of this time, but only in a half an hour of our Las Vegas time. No way of knowing.

If rescue came at all.

I pushed that thought away. I would deal with that possibility soon enough.

"Not even close to that old," Screamer said, answering my question about anyone being alive in Atlantis.

"I was born in 1930," Rocha said.

"I'm only slightly older," Katie said.

"Not even close," Patty said, smiling at me.

I always felt like the baby around gods and superheroes. This time was no exception.

Chapter Twelve

I was about to suggest that Screamer and I explore the back rooms and around the outside of the cabin when Stan appeared.

The wrong Stan.

He was standing with his back to the front door and looked to be the same Stan from our time except for one major exception. He was wearing a brown toga and brown sandals. Even in a toga, he didn't wear anything but bland colors.

"Stan!" I said before my mind processed that more than likely this wasn't the Stan from our time period.

This was the Stan looking for his daughters. More than likely the angry dad Stan who didn't know any of us from a tree.

He frowned slightly, staring at me. "Who are you?"

I knew that tone in his voice. He was already angry.

I started to open my mouth, then stopped myself when warning bells went off in the back of my head.

I glanced at Patty and then Screamer. Both had wide eyes and both were shaking their heads.

The two paramedics were standing off toward the kitchen, just watching, clearly scared but saying nothing.

If we did something wrong here, we could really, really screw up a bunch of timelines. I knew enough about time travel to know that. I just hoped that we could keep Stan under control and thinking this through.

"I don't think I can tell you," I said. "Beyond that we are from your future."

Toga-Stan started to open his mouth, then shut it and stared at me like he was trying to get a read on me.

I had no idea if there was such a thing as poker in Atlantis, which meant I had no idea what area Stan was a god in.

The silence between us grew.

I flat had no idea what to do.

But I did know that anything I did right now that was stupid would doom us to remain in the past.

"Never thought I would ever get here," Stan said from my left.

All of us spun around.

Stan from our time was there, smiling at his toga-self. He had on the same plain clothes he had been wearing earlier.

I don't think I was ever so happy to see someone. I wanted to hug him, I really did.

He looked at me. "We needed that me to arrive here so we could track where and when you exactly were," regular Stan said.

Behind the toga-Stan, Laverne and another older man with a long white beard appeared. Laverne touched toga-Stan on the shoulder. That Stan then slumped gently to the ground.

I recognized the older man with Laverne as Chronos, the God of Time. Or Father Time as many called him. But instead of white robes, he had on a silk business suit with a vest and suspenders. He looked like any really rich old guy you would see on the street.

I couldn't believe how happy I was to see him as well. But not once did the thought of hugging him cross my mind.

A moment later toga-Stan vanished.

"I find him in an hour in my office," Laverne says. "I just put a memory block on him to forget all this until he sees Nicky today in the future. That way he doesn't tell me anything."

That made a lot of sense. It protected the timeline.

Then I thought about it. She had just planted the plan to rescue us in Stan's mind to carry for over eleven thousand years while he was in the middle of rescuing us. Have I ever said how much time travel gives me a headache?

"We need to get out of here," she said.

"Hold on, we have two residents of Patty's building with us," I said.

I nodded to the two paramedics to be ready and then

instantly brought the two unconscious women to the front room. The two paramedics expertly caught the two women and held them like they did something like that every day.

"Got everyone now?" Laverne asked.

I nodded and took Patty's hand, feeling her calming influence on me.

Laverne turned to the white-bearded man who seemed to just be standing there smiling slightly as he watched like a grandfather pleased at the actions of his grandchildren.

"A ride home if you wouldn't mind, Burtram?" she asked.

Burtram Chronos? I was never getting that out of my mind.

He smiled and waved his hand.

Without even seeming to move, we were standing in front of the booth in my office that hovered over the Las Vegas Strip.

Laverne and Chronos were gone.

Stan was no longer with us either, more than likely with his daughters. I had a hunch we weren't going to be seeing him much for a time.

Around us the wonderful city of Las Vegas spread out across the desert. The sky was perfect blue, the desert perfect brown, and the planes were filling the sky on approaches to the airport. Below I could see the moving traffic and lights of The Strip.

It felt wonderful to be home.

Part of me had believed I would never see it again. Actually a very large part.

Ben and Madge were both sitting in the booth, sweating as if they had been running.

"Oh, thank heavens you are back," Ben said. "We couldn't hold this office up much longer."

I frowned and figured I would have them explain that later. It didn't feel like I was suddenly holding up the office.

Patty kissed me and then let go of my hand.

"Patty's building safe?" I asked Ben.

He nodded, using a napkin to wipe the sweat off his brow as Madge slid out of the booth and sort of staggered for the door to The Diner. "I'll get some milkshakes and fries started."

"I'll jump you two into the back area of the lobby," I said, turning to the two paramedics who were still holding up the two unconscious women residents. "From there you can get these two to the hospital."

They both nodded and I jumped them to the empty main floor of the building, thanked them for their help, and jumped back to my office.

It felt wonderful to be home.

Just wonderful.

Screamer was pulling a chair up to the booth and Patty had already slid into the side across from Ben.

"Go get Sherri," I said to Screamer as I slid into the big booth beside Patty. "Have her join us for a late lunch so we have someone to tell this story to."

He started to open his mouth, then remembered he could teleport and broke into a huge smile.

"Right back," he said, and vanished.

"Very good job today," Ben said, nodding and sipping on a glass of water in front of him. "You all saved a lot of people in a lot of timelines. How did you like Atlantis?"

"Seemed pretty advanced," I said. "But we didn't luckily see much of it."

"How are the Atlantis Fifty going to be?" Patty asked.

"The Atlantis what?" Sherri asked as she appeared with Screamer and slid into the booth as Ben slid over. "And someone want to explain to me how my husband can now teleport?"

"The Atlantis Fifty," Ben said. "They were before your time."

"Considerably," Sherri said. "If they were actually from Atlantis. I'm not that old, thank you very much."

"But we were there today," Screamer said, smiling at his wife.

"Where?" Sherrie asked, looking very puzzled.

"Atlantis," Screamer said. "Nice place, but I wouldn't want to live there. I hear it had flooding problems."

Sherri opened her mouth, staring at her husband, then shut it and looked at me.

Patty and I both laughed.

Patty finally took pity on Sherri and looked at me. "How about we start from the beginning and tell her about our day."

"Should I start with the shower part?" I asked, remembering how wonderful she looked there, naked and not moving, covered in drops of water. "With you frozen in the shower and me just staring."

"Pervert," Patty said and smacked me on the shoulder and Ben smiled like he did when amused.

"After the shower," Patty said.

"Oh, bummer," Screamer said.

And with that the laughter drained away the last of the tension I was feeling.

It was wonderful to be home, wonderful to have stopped a horrid tragedy from happening, and wonderful to be back in this time.

And even though thousands of years before in Atlantis, fifty families had been torn apart with a horrid tragedy, the Atlantis Fifty had now found a new home. They were safe and would get the help they needed.

And Stan had two daughters back he thought he'd lost forever.

All in all, I figured it was a good Saturday afternoon.

INTERNATIONAL BESTSELLING AUTHOR
DEAN WESLEY
SMITH
BEING DEAD
(THE FIRST YEAR)
A MARBLE GRANT NOVEL

SNEAK PEEK

BEING DEAD (THE FIRST YEAR)

Chapter One

Dying on a first date sucks.

Dying on a blind date sucks even worse.

Especially when your date dies with you. And then goes off through some tunnel of light into the next life or something, leaving you sitting alone, dead, in a dark alley, waiting for your own tunnel of light.

Hands down, the worst ending to any date in recorded history.

The alley we had been forced to go into was blacker than the inside of a latrine, and seeing how it smelled, I would have not been surprised to be in a latrine, but I knew I wasn't since it seemed that being dead meant I could see just fine in the dark.

And smell just fine as well. Holy crap. The nearby Chinese restaurant garbage smelled like my fridge after six days of feeling sorry for myself and laying on the couch and eating take-out without taking out the uneaten food in the original cartons. And no telling how many homeless and drunks had actually used this alley for a bathroom.

I was sitting on a big green dumpster owned by a nearby office, so thankfully it didn't have the odor of the other dumpsters coming up between my legs.

The scum with the greasy black hair and dirty ski parka that had killed us was going through my date's pockets as I sat and watched.

The guy looked skinny and no doubt drug-addicted. His motions were jerky, his eyes darting around him like a rat trying to find a way out of a maze.

My blind date, dear old Handsome Bob, as I had started to think of him for the full thirty minutes I had known him, had caused this mess by thinking he could be a macho asshole or something.

The scum with the greasy black hair had approached us on the sidewalk and Bob had shaken his head and said, "Not now."

We were headed down the street to a nice Italian restaurant that served the best red wine and bread plate this side of New York. And that was going some for the Old Towne section of Boise, Idaho.

Bob was dressed in a clearly expensive silk suit and no tie, while I didn't look so cheap myself. For the date I had put on dark slacks, a white silk blouse with pearls around my neck, and a thin see-through sweater. No bra because I wanted my date to get an occasional peek at what might be offered after dinner if things went right.

Sitting dead in an alley sure wasn't my idea of things going right.

The greasy jerk had pulled out a gun, his hands shaking. Dear old dead Handsome Bob had said, "You don't want to do that."

Bless him.

Clearly the druggie did want to do exactly what he was doing, but I didn't say that. I was busy ramping up one of my super powers.

You see, before I was so suddenly cut down, I had worked as a superhero in the housing and hotel industry. Over the last century I had worked both front desks of hotels and sold real estate. At the moment I was on the real estate side, trying to help out in the booming Boise real estate market.

Amazing the kind of crap that goes on in real estate when big money is involved.

I hit greasy-hair with a full dose of my calming power. The guy was so high on drugs my power actually didn't do anything but make him stop shaking so hard.

He pointed to the dark alley with the gun. "Get in there and then dig out your money."

"And if we say no?" Handsome Bob asked the guy.

Since Bob was almost a foot taller than the greasy-haired druggie, I suppose Bob thought he could bully the situation a little.

Bless dear old now-dead stupid Bob.

I hit the guy with another dose of calming power. I had enough power on a normal day to stop a shouting, irate, pissed-off hotel customer at a front desk and make them smile.

The guy with the gun got calmer, but his pea brain was still set on robbing us. At least I got him to not shoot us right there on the sidewalk because of Handsome Bob's stupidity.

"Let's just give him our stuff and he will let us go," I said to Bob.

"Smart woman," the guy said, smiling and showing a mouthful of rotted teeth.

Actually, I had planned that when we got into the alley I would simply jump us away from this nut and then figure out something to tell dear old Bob.

Bob didn't know I was a one-hundred-year-old superhero and could just teleport anywhere I wanted. Not something you tell someone before a first blind date. Men tended to have sexual problems when they realized the woman they were with was over a hundred.

Bob nodded to me and we walked the twenty steps into the alley, Bob pushing me slightly ahead of him.

Then, as we stopped and turned at just about the point where the rotted Chinese food odor got the worst, Bob went to lunge at the guy.

Handsome Bob went to really, really stupid Bob very quickly.

I was so surprised Bob would do something that idiotic, I didn't react fast enough to jump us out of there.

The guy fired, hitting Bob in the arm.

The bullet went through Bob's flesh and hit me square between the eyes.

Now that was a shocker, let me tell you.

One moment I am standing alive in the alley and the next I am a ghost sitting on a smelly dumpster watching dear old Handsome Bob hold his arm and swear.

The greasy-haired guy was now twitching again. He stared at my body lying there in the alley, clearly getting my wonderful blouse and sweater all stained up with my own blood.

Then he looked at Bob, who was also staring at me, holding his wounded arm and looking sick to his stomach.

Then the guy did what any self-respecting murderer would do. He shot Bob.

Bob slumped to the ground and the guy fired one more shot into Bob's head.

A moment later I watched Bob's ghost stand up, look around, then look up and float off into a white light.

"Nice meeting you jerk-face," I shouted after Bob.

I was pretty sure he didn't hear me.

As I said, the worst ending to a blind date ever.

Chapter Two

The druggie who had killed me and my blind date started through Bob's pockets. The druggie pulled out a money clip and then took Bob's watch. Then he rolled Bob over slightly and took out his wallet.

He pulled out a single-package condom and tossed it aside.

I just shook my head. "Damn, Bob, only one? Where was the confidence? If you had come back to my place, you would have needed at least three just to make it to breakfast."

The greasy murderer clearly didn't hear me. And I had a hunch dead Bob didn't either.

I glanced around. I was still the only ghost in the alley.

Where was my greeting party?

I figured I had become a Ghost Agent, which was why I hadn't gotten the beam-of-light ride. I had never met a Ghost

Agent, but I had heard from my best friend Patty that she and her boyfriend, Poker Boy, had worked with some Ghost Agents just lately to save the world. Seems Patty and her boyfriend were always saving the world, which I must admit I appreciated.

The guy stood and stepped toward my body.

"Hey, not so fast there, jerk-face," I said, jumping down from the dumpster and brushing off my pants.

The greasy-haired slime-ball picked up my clutch purse and went through it. That I didn't much care about. I had a few hundred in there and that was that.

But then he looked around at the mouth of the alley and then looked back at me with that look I had seen scum like him get. Ghost or no ghost, he wasn't touching me, even if I did have a hole in the middle of my forehead.

This night had gone bad enough as it was.

The guy kneeled down beside my body and I took two quick steps at the guy and went to kick him clear across the alley.

Foot went right through him. Charlie Brown would have been proud of my form, though. I didn't end up on my back.

However, when my foot went through the guy, I got to read all of his thoughts.

All of what he was about to do to me.

So I closed my eyes and went inside the scum. Now I knew for a fact I was in a cesspool, swimming in the shit that this guy called thoughts. If I got out of here I would need about ten showers.

If ghosts took showers.

As he reached for my right breast, I shouted at the top of my lungs, "No!"

And trust me, I can be loud.

Just ask anyone who sat beside me at a Broncos' football game.

And I was inside the guy when I shouted.

Slime-bucket grabbed his head and rolled over backward, the intense pain striking everywhere.

As he rolled away, I managed to stand my ground and get out of his body. I shook myself, wishing I could forget the memories of what I had just seen in his mind.

It would take twenty showers before I would feel clean again.

The guy was holding his head and screaming and rolling on the ground. Blood was coming out of his ears.

Both ears.

"Wow, what did you do to him?" a voice behind me asked.

I turned around to see a handsome couple standing to one side looking shocked. Both were about my height of five-ten, both wore jeans, expensive shirts, and tennis shoes.

"The pervert was about to get his jollies on my dead body, so I climbed inside his head and shouted as loud as I could."

Both of them laughed.

Then the woman stepped forward. "I'm Jewel and this is Tommy. We came to help get you used to being a ghost, but guess you are doing just fine."

I shook both their hands, happy as hell I had company.

"I'm Marble Grant. And got a hunch I'm going to need a lot of help."

"Someone close to you?" Tommy asked, pointing at Handsome Bob.

"Knew him for thirty minutes," I said. "Blind date. But I had planned on getting much closer to him after dinner, if you get my drift."

Jewel laughed and Tommy actually blushed a little, which I loved. I had a feeling I was going to like these two.

"I suppose you two are Ghost Agents. Right?"

Both of them looked shocked.

"I was a superhero in the hospitality and real estate side of the world," I said. "Any chance you two know Patty Ledgerwood and Poker Boy?"

"We do," Jewel said.

"You know," I said, "I'm damn hungry and I assume there is a way ghosts eat, so any chance we could get out of this smell and grab a bite and you guys call Patty and have her meet us. I would kind of like to tell her about my sudden death myself, since she has been my best friend for a hundred years now, give or take."

Both of them just nodded.

"Anything we need to do with that guy?" I asked, looking down at the scum who had killed me and Handsome Bob before I had the chance to find out if the handsome part went all the way to Bob's southern regions.

Greasy hair was still rolling on the dirty concrete, holding his ears and screaming. He was losing a lot of blood through his fingers. I clearly had done some damage.

"I think he's finished," Tommy said, laughing.

"Yeah," Jewel said. "Got to remember that trick."

With that we jumped to a place I knew well and loved, the Golden Nugget Buffet in downtown Las Vegas.

Now I knew I was really going to like these two.

CHAPTER THREE

The Golden Nugget Buffet had been decorated in all warm brown cloth and polished brass. Plants ringed the outside of the side part of the dining room nearest the escalator and the tables were solid, as were the chairs.

My hand went right through a chair as I tried to pull it out and Jewel did it for me.

"You'll learn how to actually move some physical matter, but you don't want to do that too often because people start to get spooked."

"I'll bet," I said.

Tommy jumped away to find Patty, and Jewel led me up to the wonderful smelling food. The images from the murderer's head were slowly fading, something I was very grateful for.

"Be careful to not run into anyone," Jewel said, indicating the six people around the large buffet area. "You end up reading their thoughts."

"Yeah, learned that with the guy who shot me," I said.

Jewel showed me how to pick up a plate, which was actually just the ghost component of the plate, and how to take food from the buffet.

In five minutes of filling a ghost plate with ghost food, I managed to not run into anyone alive, which sort of felt like a victory. I called it the dance of the living. A living person came toward me, I stepped sideways and went around them.

Jewel did the same, seemingly without noticing.

Back at the table, I bit into a piece of prime rib and damn near had an orgasm right there at the table.

Jewel just smiled as I moaned and kept on eating the fantastic tasting food.

"I remember the food being good here," I said after a few bites, "but never this good."

"Everything is better when you are a ghost," Jewel said. "Food tastes better, emotions are more powerful, and the travel and living is easier."

"Sex?" I asked.

"As the joke goes," Jewel said, smiling, "it's to die for."

"Oh, no," I said. "I had enough trouble controlling myself when I was alive."

Jewel just laughed and at that moment Tommy appeared.

"Patty is in Poker Boy's office," Tommy said. "Let's just

grab some food and jump there. She's expecting us but doesn't know why yet."

It dawned on me why Patty couldn't jump here. She was still alive. Anyone in the restaurant would see her arrive and then talk to no one. Not a good idea.

Tommy headed for the buffet. I really needed to pee, but instead I kept eating as we waited for him. Damn, the food was so good. I was going to be lucky to not gain a ton of weight now that I had died. I needed to remember to ask Jewel and Tommy how they stayed so thin.

After Tommy came back with a full plate of food, he jumped the three of us and our food and drink to what I assumed was Poker Boy's office, although I had never been there.

In fact, the place was like a legend.

But I had heard it was something special and I had heard right. The office wasn't really an office. It was more like a tile platform floating in the air a thousand feet over the Strip.

All four walls were freaking clear glass with a wood railing about waist high all the way around.

Without that railing, I would have been so afraid of falling off that slick checkered tile floor, I would have been clinging to the furniture and screaming like a ten-year-old girl not wanting to go see her uncle.

And I was dead, so pretty certain the fall wouldn't kill me again.

Still, scary damn place and now I really had to pee.

I made my heart stop racing and looked around.

In the very center of the room was this huge 1950s style diner booth, with a scarred tabletop and red vinyl booth seats on three sides. The thing was big enough to hold ten people if the people really liked each other.

There were half-a-dozen chairs around the room that could be pulled up to the open end of the booth I suppose, but three of them just sat facing out over the incredible view of the city.

And wow, what a view. I had always loved the lights of Las Vegas. Just never seen them from the air like this before.

"Marble," Patty said as we appeared. "Tommy said you needed to talk with me. Everything all right? You could have just called you know?"

"Not sure I knew how exactly," I said, smiling at my best friend.

Jewel laughed as she set her food and mine on the booth table.

Patty was wearing her MGM Grand Front Desk uniform of dark slacks, tan blouse and a lighter tan vest. She had her long hair pulled back and was as stunning as ever.

Patty frowned, something I had rarely seen her do in a century.

I glanced at my food on the booth table, then turned back to my friend. "Got myself killed while on a blind date about thirty minutes ago."

Patty's eyes went totally round. "Are you all right?"

"Pretty sure I'm dead," I said, laughing. I pointed to my forehead. "Bullet right there did the trick."

Patty looked like she was about to cry.

"Can I hug her?" I asked, glancing back at Jewel.

"She's a superhero," Jewel said, "and she can see you, so sure, don't know why not?"

I stepped toward Patty and she hugged me so hard, I wasn't sure I would be able to breathe.

And I hugged her back.

I guess, for the first time, it was sinking in that I had really died.

I was still here but I was dead.

That just sucked.

Except for the part about the food tasting so much better.

Finish Reading
Being Dead (The First Year): A Marble Grant Novel

**Go to
MARBLEGRANT.com**

Get More Marble Grant

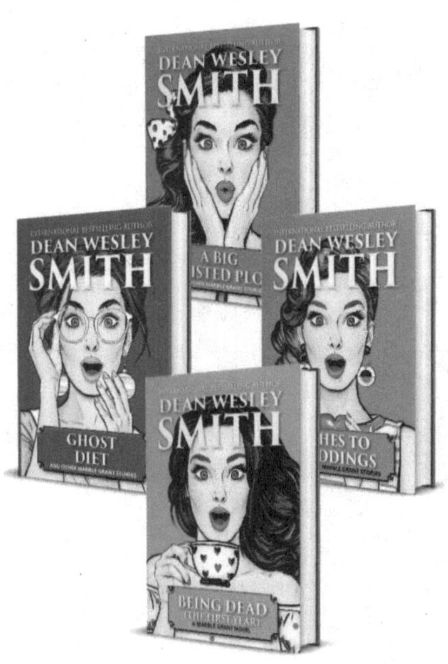

DeanWesleySmithStore.com

Hear From Dean

Want More From Dean?

For Dean Wesley Smith's newsletter
go to deanwesleysmith.com.

Get the latest news and releases from all of WMG's authors
and lines, including Kristine Grayson, Kris Nelscott,
Pulphouse Magazine, and so much more...

To sign up, **go to wmgbooks.com.**

About the Author
Dean Wesley Smith

Considered one of the most prolific writers working in modern fiction, *New York Times* and *USA Today* bestselling writer, Dean Wesley Smith published over two hundred novels and over seven hundred books in forty years, and hundreds and hundreds of short stories. He has over thirty million copies of his books in print.

At the moment he produces novels in four major series, including the time travel **Thunder Mountain** novels set in the old west, the galaxy-spanning **Seeders Universe** series, the cold case mystery series, **Cold Poker Gang** series, and the superhero series staring **Poker Boy.**

During his career, Dean also wrote a couple dozen *Star Trek* novels, the only two original *Men in Black* novels, Spider-Man and X-Men novels, plus novels set in gaming and television worlds. Writing with his wife Kristine Kathryn Rusch under the name Kathryn Wesley, they wrote the novel for the NBC miniseries **The Tenth Kingdom** and other books for *Hallmark Hall of Fame* movies.

He wrote novels under dozens of pen names in the worlds

of comic books and movies, including novelizations of almost a dozen films, from *X-Men* to *The Final Fantasy* to *Steel* to *Rundown*.

Dean also worked as a fiction editor off and on, starting at Pulphouse Publishing, then at *VB Tech Journal*, then Pocket Books, and now at WMG Publishing where he and Kristine Kathryn Rusch serve as executive editors for the acclaimed *Fiction River* anthology series. He took over the editorship of the acclaimed *Pulphouse Magazine* in 2018.

For more information about Dean's books and ongoing projects, please visit his website at www.deanwesleysmith.com

facebook.com/deanwsmith3

patreon.com/deanwesleysmith

bookbub.com/authors/dean-wesley-smith